MW01047816

Acknowledgements

First and foremost, I must acknowledge my wife, Patty. You have been a great writing partner, story collaborator, editor, and muse. I appreciate that you see the world so differently than I. That difference keeps me on my toes. You have made the entire writing and living processes fun.

Not On MY Watch

By Jeff Bailey

NOT ON MY WATCH is published by:
Deer Hawk Publishing, an imprint of Deer
Hawk Enterprises
www.deerhawkpublications.com

Cover design by:
Raymond Polizzi

Layout by:
Aurelia Sands

Library of Congress Control Number:
9781625969774

Chapter One

The burning metal airframe superstructure hissed at Cassie. The cockpit of a fighter jet was tight to begin with, but once it was crumpled in a crash, it was almost too snug to allow her to take a deep breath. The heat was unbearable. She inched forward, feeling her way through the swirling smoke and trying to use her diaphragm and stomach to draw her breath instead of expanding her lungs. The roar of the flames overstimulated her hearing until all sound faded to white noise. She blew out a breath and pulled herself further into the burning structure. She tried to orient herself each time the occasional flashes of light from the flames penetrated the smoke enough for her to see shadows.

Cassie, Lance Corporal Cassandra Sing, USMC, estimated that one more squeeze into the void would bring her close enough to the pilot to feel for his body. An explosion sounded nearby, shaking the structure. The metal casement seemed to close in even tighter, intensifying her claustrophobia. The explosion also added to her sense of urgency. As if aviation fire rescue wasn't dangerous enough, Cassie was a US Marine aviation fire rescue specialist. When she fought

1

an airplane fire or rescued a pilot, there was the possibility of live bullets and bombs in the plane. The explosion meant that she had to hurry. Burning flight fuel, bullets, and bombs don't play well together.

Cassie maneuvered onto her side and reached forward with her free hand, making it even harder to draw a breath. But her effort was rewarded. She felt the slack face of the Marine pilot just out of sight in the darkness. She pulled the small rescue-breathing mask from the Velcro connector on the shoulder of her canvas fire jacket and fitted it over the pilot's face. Procedures dictated that she first protect the pilot's ability to breathe whenever there was a possible nuclear weapon or nuclear material onboard the aircraft. Aspirated radioactive metals wreak havoc on the human body. With the mask in place, she reached back down to her waist, retrieved her field knife, and cut the pilot free of his harness. The heat was beginning to leach through her fire jacket.

The pilot fell against Cassie like a sack of wet sand and pinned her head against the metal structure. The loss of that tiny bit of space compounded her growing claustrophobia. Another small shot of panic coursed through her as the adrenaline hit her blood stream. She couldn't suppress a little scream. The roar of the fire consumed the sound. She could not give in to panic. A fellow Marine's life was at stake. She would not falter.

After blowing out another breath, she inched her way back out the way she entered, pulling the deadweight of the pilot behind her. *Breathe, scoot, pull, breathe, scoot, pull.* She had a long way to go.

As she moved, she heard the report of an incredibly loud Claxton horn from somewhere outside the burning fuselage. The flames stopped with a whispered, final puff. The smoke swirled away. The recorded roar of the fire stopped. The metal fuselage lifted off her from above and pivoted away on hinges. In relief, Cassie took a quick, deep breath. She, and the pilot next to her, turned to look up at the cloudless, blue sky above them. Both pulled off their breathing apparatus and turned their attention to the fire training NCO standing over them.

The sergeant gave one short order, "I'm terminating this confined-spaces exercise. Corporal Sing, fall in with the rest of your class."

As the NCO turned back to the rest of the class, the acting pilot jumped up and offered Cassie a hand up, which she accepted.

As he pulled her to her feet, he said with real sincerity, "Thanks for saving my butt today, Marine."

He put his fist out at chest level. Cassie reached up to her eye level, fist bumped the offered compliment, and replied with an "Oorah." Lance Corporal Cassandra Sing was not only smaller than most Marines, at five foot four, she was smaller than most female Marines. After the bump, she pulled her fist away quickly. She didn't want anyone to see that her hands were still shaking.

As she took her place in ranks with her class, she dropped her fire helmet and air pack at her feet and waited for the members of the class to settle down. She also did a quick scan of the surrounding area (Marine training becomes instinctive) The fire-training facility looked like the open tarmac of a major airport: flat, hard, and barren of anything living or flammable. It seemed like she could see forever. The open countryside of Central Oklahoma was the perfect location for a military fire-training center. The nuclear weapons facilities on the other side of the base made it ideal for a nuclear materials fire-training center.

Cassie's class consisted of firefighters from all five branches of the service. Some were aviation fire fighters like her. Others were trained shipboard, submarine, and even structural firefighters. The students at the school included pilots who might fly a plane with a nuclear weapon on board, medics who might treat Americans exposed to radiation, RadCon (Radiation Control) technicians who might evaluate an area or building for radiation safety, bomb squad specialists who might neutralize a nuclear weapon, and firefighters who might fight a nuclear-weapon-involved aviation fire. They all had one thing in common. They were all on assigned temporary duty at the Fort Sill Nuclear Weapons Depot to learn to fight a fire when nuclear materials or nuclear weapons might be present.

Three men in uniform stood in front of the class. One was the training NCO, dressed in Army utilities, who supervised the day-to-day instruction. The second was the commanding officer of the training facility. He wore an immaculate, khaki office uniform. The third man was an Army officer, but he wore a stereotypical civilian fire captain's uniform.

The class training NCO spoke up. "We're suspending the training schedule for the rest of the afternoon. Class will resume at zero seven hundred tomorrow in classroom six. Read chapter five in your training manual, Elements of Radiation Detection. There may be quiz at the start of class tomorrow. This is Base Fire Marshall McDermott. Listen up!"

The Fire Marshall didn't waste any words. "Ladies and gentlemen, we have a situation. We have an expanding grass fire on the north perimeter of the base. Normally, we only monitor a grass fire as long as it doesn't threaten any structures or lives. This fire is approaching the perimeter fence, which means that it is going to spread into the surrounding civilian countryside. That's unacceptable. The base commander has authorized me to mobilize this fire-training class to assist the base fire brigade to fight this fire."

Fire Marshall McDermott realized for the first time that Cassie was wearing desert style utility boots. He stopped addressing the class and focused on her, "Marine, where are your fire boots?"

Cassie snapped to attention, "Sir, the fire training locker does not have regulation fire boots in my size. I have special permission to train in utilities."

McDermott considered this for a moment then said, "Very well, but you will avoid hot spots, is that clear."

"Clear, sir."

McDermott turned back to the class, "It's time to stretch your legs, get dirty, and fight a real fire. Report to the equipment locker room and equipment-up for a grass fire. Fall in at the staging area in ten minutes."

McDermott did a sharp about-face and started a conversation with the Training officer.

The training NCO stepped up and shouted, "Fall out!"

Two minutes later, the firefighters entered the equipment room.

A sailor walking next to Cassie said, "You got balls of steel, Sing. That confined-spaces exercise bothers the hell out of me."

Cassie offered a fist-bump and an 'Oorah' as before. She lowered her hand and checked it: stone solid - nice. Cassie was already dressed in the required canvas bibs and jacket. She put her helmet and breathing apparatus in the locker. She wouldn't need them on the grassfire. The only other item of a fire uniform that she needed was real fire boots.

Before leaving her locker, Cassie checked her phone for messages. She never carried her phone when she was on duty. She learned that lesson the hard way; two smashed phones, one melted phone, and three lost phones in a year. She couldn't afford to keep buying phones. On her way out of the equipment locker, she picked up a walkie-talkie and clipped it to the epaulette of her jacket.

Chapter Two

As Cassie and the fire crews were on their way to fight the grass fire north of the base, Susan Wajowski sat in her SUV in a line of cars waiting to enter Fort Sill's South gate, the main gate. Susan was a civilian employee at the Weapons Logistics Command on base. As such, she had limited base privileges when she wasn't on duty, and she wasn't on duty today. Her soon to be ex-husband, Theodore Wajowski (Teddy or Flea) sat next to her in the passenger seat. A few of his Army friends called him Teddy. Everybody else called him *Flea* because *Rat Puke* was too noble a nickname for him. "Flea" was the nickname that Teddy's mother gave him as a child because he was smaller and weaker than the other boys. She used the name when she wanted to ridicule, belittle, or shut the boy down and never missed an opportunity to break out in peals of laughter at his discomfort. She knew that belittling Flea would cause him to withdraw and allow her to return to her cherished hard drugs and drinking. Flea never knew his father.

Flea was no longer in the Army. He had been out for less than a month. Before the Army discharged Flea, he managed to *lose* his ID and had to get a replacement. The day he processed out, he turned in the replacement, but pocketed the original. A valid military ID can come in handy.

As she waited, Susan stole a glance at the two men in the back seat. She had never seen either of them before today. That notwithstanding, she didn't like them. They were her husband's scumbag friends.

One was tall had a flattop haircut and looked like a white supremacy, psycho-killer. Flat Top was always staring at her. His eyes looked like he would enjoy hurting her. Flea introduced the other man as The Major. He didn't look like he was now, or ever had been, in the military. She thought that he looked like a fast-talking con artist. Maybe Flea called him The Major because he wore a ratty, second-hand Army fatigue coat with Major's gold oak leaf insignia on it. Of course, the insignia were in the wrong place on the coat. The man was a joke, a wannabe.

No, she didn't like these men, her soon-to-be ex-husband included.

She rolled her car forward a little. She was now the third car from the gate.

Flea broke the strained silence, "Just be cool, Susan. It'll all be over in an hour or so and then I'll give you the papers. Don't screw this up. Smile, you're having fun."

The line of cars rolled forward, again. Flea turned to the men in back, "Take your driver's licenses out of your wallets, and hand them to the MP when he asks for them. Look straight at him until he verifies your ID and hands your licenses back. I'll show him my military ID. It's sweet little Susan's windshield sticker that will get us on base."

Flea grinned his stupid, rat puke grin.

The car in front of Susan pulled away. It was Susan's turn in front of the MP.

She smiled and shielded her eyes from the afternoon sun, "Good morning, ah, afternoon."

"Good afternoon, Ma'am." He looked at the base sticker on Susan's windshield, then at Susan. If she were alone, the MP would have waved her through without a glance. The three passengers required that he ask a question or two to make sure that Susan wasn't under any duress.

"What is your business on Fort Sill, today, Ma'am?"

"We're going to get a bite to eat at the PX and then go to a movie."

The MP smiled at Susan, glanced at Fleas ID, and then turned his attention to the men in the back seat, "ID's, gentlemen?" He compared the pictures on the IDs with the faces of the men. He checked the expiration dates on the licenses.

Then the MP startled Susan. He looked back to Flat Top as though he had found something suspicious. Flat Top didn't flinch. After a second, the MP handed the IDs back, "Thank you, gentlemen."

He stepped back from Susan's car, waived her forward, and said, "Enjoy the movie, ma'am."

Susan drove onto Fort Sill like it was just a normal day.

As Susan dove around the base, the men each pulled a small duffle from under their feet. They changed into Army uniforms. Flat Top dressed as a First Lieutenant. He looked the part, supremely arrogant, absurdly self-absorbed, and ready to verbally assault anyone who challenged his absolute authority. He would play the part of being in charge during today's excursion.

The Major impersonated a Sargent First Class. He also looked the part, as if he was accustomed to supervising the day-to-day work of the Army. After all, he was the leader of this little so-called *Americans Constitutional Reform* movement.

Flea put on one of his old uniforms. He was used to being a private, a grunt.

"Drive us over to the motor pool. Stop at the corner across the street." Flea ordered.

A few minutes later, Susan pulled her car to the curb outside the motor pool. She took a manila envelope out from under her seat and held it out toward Flea.

When he reached for it, she pulled it back, "Un uh."

Flea glared at her with obvious disgust. He hated the way she had of displaying her distrust of his every action. After a moment, he took a bundle of papers from his Army tote and shoved them at Susan.

"Okay, there, all signed. You get everything, including full custody of the kids just like you wanted." His words carried the implied title of *Bitch*, even if he didn't say it.

Susan took the papers and put them between the driver's door and seat. After today, you're out of my life forever. Don't contact me. Don't try to see the kids, nothing. It wouldn't be fair to them. I mean it, no contact ever!"

"Yeah, Yeah," Flea snatched the envelope and shoved it into his tote.

"Make sure you destroy those papers when you're done. They can lead back to me."

"Up yours."

"Teddy, destroy them."

"Okay, okay, I will. I'm going to go check out a truck. Drive around for a half hour then meet me at the baseball diamonds."

Susan stole a glance at the men in the back seat who were enjoying the intimate exchange in the front seat. "Can't they go with you or wait on the corner or something?"

"Officers and sergeants don't go with privates to check a vehicle out of the motor pool. And, no, they can't wait on the corner. We're on a military base. Everyone outside is going somewhere with purpose. No one just lingers around. Someone might notice. Just drive around for a few minutes, would ya?"

Flea got out and walked toward the motor pool.

Nothing more was said in the car as Susan pulled away from the curb.

Flat Top leered.

At the checkout desk, the motor sergeant looked at the orders. He didn't ask for Flea's military ID because Flea had checked out vehicles in the recent past. Checking an

Army vehicle out of the motor pool with a proper set of orders was little more difficult than checking a book out of a library with a valid library card. The difference was that the motor sergeant was required to inspect the truck for roadworthiness and sign a vehicle release pass before the requesting driver could take his vehicle out of the motor pool. It took Flea twenty minutes to check all the fluid levels and the tire pressure. He washed the windows, cleaned the battery terminals, and swept out the cab of the truck. Finally, the sergeant signed Flea's pass and Flea drove his two and a half ton Army cargo truck off the motor pool grounds. A few minutes later, he parked behind Susan at the baseball fields.

The Major and Flat Top got out of Susan's car without a word, took the three tote bags, and got in with Flea. As The Major and Flat Top stowed their bags behind the bench seat, Flea took one last opportunity to flip off Susan. The effort was wasted. Susan was already driving away and never looked back.

Next stop, the Fourth Army Specialized Ordinance Maintenance Facility.

Chapter Three

At the same moment, the three con-spirators were driving to the weapons center, Cassie and the other firefighters were hard at work cutting a firebreak across the prairie north of the base. Cutting a firebreak with shovels and hoes under the Oklahoma sun was grueling. The fire fighters worked at a frantic pace, each trying to outwork the others. Cassie was able to hold her own.

Needling banter helped.

A Navy firefighter called out, "Hey, Woody, you going to NCO Club for a few beers after this walk in the park or are you going to study for the big quiz?"

Cassie answered for the man, "He's going to study. You know Air Force pukes can't drink."

Without looking up Woody retorted in his best playground voice, "Drink your butt under the table, Sing."

A voice from down the fire line called, "No one's getting a brew until we knock this fire down. Try to keep up."

A huge bear of a seaman pushed his way into the fire line next to Cassie and growled, "Correcto." so get your lazy butt out of my way so a Navy firefighter can show you how it's done."

The first fire fighter chimed back in, "Yeah, c'mon, Woody, you and Sing might have some fun. It's ladies' night."

Cassie tried to blow sweat on the man as she answered, "Bite me, Miles!"

Cassie stepped back for moment, pulled a water bottle out of her canvas bibs and took a long drink. She was about to take a second when someone called to her to quit screwing around and get back to work. Hoots and laughter were the fire line response.

Cassie loved it.

So went the next several hours.

Chapter Four

The next stop for the three men was the Fourth Army Specialized Ordinance Maintenance Facility. Flea expected even less scrutiny at the maintenance facility because he didn't have to perform any maintenance on the nuclear weapons before he checked them out. The nuclear weapons maintenance specialists at the facility performed the required maintenance. All Flea needed was a valid set of transport orders.

Under normal operating conditions, nuclear weapons arrived at the maintenance facility on rail cars. After the required maintenance or repair, most of the weapons shipped back out on the rail system to the Army or Air Force base of origin. On rare occasions, the Army retired a weapon and shipped it by truck to a long-term storage facility in the empty expanse of grasslands on the western edge of the main base. Maintenance facility personnel had their copy of a valid set of paperwork and were expecting a shipment to go out today.

Two copies of the same order were required to release a weapon from the maintenance facility regardless of the destination. Weapons Logistics Command sent one set of orders to the maintenance facility and an identical copy to the designated carrier through different administrative channels.

When an authorized carrier, such as an Army specialist with an Army truck, presented a valid copy of a transport order, the shipping control officer compared the shipper's copy to the one received at the facility. If the copies matched, the shipping control officer released the cargo to the shipper. The shipping control officer at the receiving facility followed the same procedure. If the documents matched, the shipping officer accepted the shipment.

Thanks to Susan, Flea possessed a forged copy of an order authorizing the release of two nuclear weapons for transport to long-term storage. Flea's orders matched the copy at the facility.

The next part of the operation was a little dicey. The three men had orally rehearsed the sequence a hundred times. If each played his part, looked his part, and kept to the plan, they might just pull it off. Every movement, every blink of an eye was meticulously choreographed.

With The Major (now a sergeant) in the middle and Flat Top (now an officer) riding shotgun, Flea (once again a private) drove up to the maintenance facility guard shack. Flat Top took the orders out of the envelope and handed them to Flea, who handed them to the guard. The guard sent them into the facility office via pneumatic tube and then seemed to be trying to stare through the three men in the truck.

Once facility personnel verified the orders, a little green light lit up on the guard's control console. They were in. The gate opened and Flea drove to the loading dock entrance.

The facility loading dock was just like any loading dock at any commercial trucking center, with a few noticeable exceptions. One, it was indoors, was immaculate, was painted a perfect dull grey, and was bleak and sterile. The presence of guards armed with automatic rifles was also a little different. Maybe, it wasn't exactly like a civilian loading dock.

When the doors opened, Flea drove into the bay and backed up to the loading dock. Flat Top was an officer and officers supervise. When the truck stopped, Flat Top got out, walked up the stairs at the end of the loading dock, and went into the Day Room. The Day Room (waiting room) was as stark and uninviting as Flea said it was, a ratty couch, a small table, and a coffee pot with stale coffee. Flat Top poured himself a cup of coffee and took up a position looking out the small Day Room window at the loading dock. He tried his best to look imposing, unapproachable, and someone not bent on conversation. Everyone gave him a wide berth.

The Major got out of the truck, also walked up the stairs but stayed on the platform. His job was to pretend to be verifying that the cargo was loaded and secured. Unfortunately, The Major wouldn't have recognized a 'correctly loaded and secured' cargo if he tried. He was supposed to look competent but say nothing. The facility crew would load and secure the cargo.

After a few anxious minutes, a set of doors opened and several men in bright yellow coveralls pushed their cargo out onto the dock and onto the truck. The cold-war era weapons were the size of a small chest freezer and were mounted in shipping frames but didn't have their distinctive metal covers installed. The transfer was not going off base so there was no need to conceal the contents from the public. There was also no need for a guard detail.

The transfer crew was enough. The facility people went about their task of loading and strapping down the cargo. The Major looked like he knew the process. Flat Top continued to look like an ass hole.

Flea got out of the truck and went into the transfer office to retrieve three dosimeters. After all, they were transferring nuclear weapons. As he was filling out the required form, someone walked up behind him.

"Teddy, what are you doing here? I thought they discharged you?"

Flea froze. He turned and recognized one of his casual friends, a radiation control NCO named LaBarge. LaBarge didn't seem surprised to see Flea, so Flea relaxed.

"Nah. They're trying to, and I can't wait, but they extended me a few weeks over some snafu or another. I think they're just trying to squeeze as much work out of me as they can. You know the Army."

"Yeah, that sounds like the Army. Well, stay cool man and don't get into any trouble. You're close, man. You don't want to fubar it now."

"Right, you too. Don't work too hard."

"Never. Gotta run. I have dosimeter replacement rounds, again. See ya."

"Yeah, see ya." Flea watched La-Barge leave just to make sure that he wasn't alerted to something wrong.

After LaBarge was out of sight, Flea took a dosimeter to The Major who clipped it on his breast pocket cover. He also took one to Flat Top who also clipped it on his pocket. All Flea had to do now was get back in the truck. As he stepped up onto the running board, LaBarge and facility security guard came out a small side door. They walked down the dock to within a few feet of Flea's truck. The Major started to react, but Flea waved him off. The men passed Flea without acknowledging him and walked to another loading slot. Another truck was pulling in. Flea sighed and sat down in the driver's seat. The Major went back to looking official.

The weapons were secure. A couple of yellow-suits approached The Major and they started signing the transfer papers.

Flea looked in the direction of the Day Room. Flat Top was coming out right on cue. He joined the group of signers. No one said a word, good. The yellow-suits just wanted to get back to whatever it was that they were doing before this interruption. Transfers like this one were all too routine and more than a little boring, good.

After everything was signed and initialed, copies were distributed. The yellow-suits expected Flat Top to take a bundle of the copies with him to turn into the long-term storage facility. All done, Flat Top and The Major got back into the truck.

Now, came the easy part, all they had to do was drive out. Automatic doors and gates would open before them. It was over.

Had this been a normal shipment, Flea would have driven to the long-term storage facility and presented his copy of the order, same as before. But this wasn't a normal shipment. Flea wasn't going to the storage facility. By tomorrow morning, some duty sergeant in the receiving office at the storage facility would realize that he had an order authorizing the receipt of two nuclear weapons for long-term storage, and that no weapons had been received. Susan wasn't able to stop the transmission of this third set of orders. Of course, Flea and his companions planned to be far, far away by the time the discrepancy was detected.

Flea, The Major, and Flat Top would just drive aimlessly around the base and, at the low traffic time around sunset, leave by the deserted north gate.

Chapter Five

At dusk, the amalgamated fire crew was mopping up the last remnants of the grass fire. Cassie was collecting tools at the far eastern end of the fire line. Night was falling over the grassy foothills. Cassie could still see a small crescent of the sun on the western horizon, but the panorama of stars was already becoming visible. The stars fascinated Cassie. They were like an image from a dream displayed in real life. She didn't see stars like this in southern California where she grew up; there was too much light pollution.

*****

At the same moment Cassie first saw the cargo truck at the Fort Sill north entrance, Teddy Wajowski, 'Flea,' was sitting in the middle of the truck's bench seat. "Flea" was the nickname that Teddy's mother gave him as a child because he was smaller and weaker than the other boys. She used the name when she wanted to ridicule, belittle, or shut the boy down and never missed an opportunity to break out in peals of laughter at his discomfort. She knew that belittling Flea would cause him to withdraw and allow her to return to her cherished hard drugs and drinking. Flea never knew his father.

Flea didn't have a part to play at the Fort Sill back gate: the two men seated on either side of him would get them through. Flat Top was driving.

If this shipment was scheduled to leave Fort Sill by truck, a third copy of the shipping order would have been transmitted to the military police barracks and then to the gate through official channels. This wasn't an authorized shipment. There would be no third copy of the orders at the gate. All three men in the deuce and a half knew that they would have to force their way through the gate.

The main gate that they had used to come on base was too crowded. There were too many soldiers and too many armed military police in the area. They had to leave Fort Sill by the nice quiet north gate.

Flat Top oversaw this phase of the operation because this was the kind of work at which Flat Top excelled. The Major pulled one of the carryall bags off the floor and distributed three automatic pistols equipped with silencers and extended magazines attached. After driving around for two hours to waste time until dusk when traffic would be lightest, Flat Top turned toward the back gate. Flea started hyperventilating the closer they got to the gate. He was more than a little nervous. He wasn't a hardened criminal like Flat Top. He'd never killed before, like Flat Top. He didn't know what to expect. Flat Top stopped a full twenty feet away from the gate's stop line, as planned.

As the deuce approached the north gate, Flea, now in the middle, reached up and turned on the small RF jammer that was sitting on the dash. Ft. Sill MP headquarters went blind to the events at the north gate. Flat Top was driving. The Major was on the right. Both had their silenced automatic pistols ready.

*****

Cassie dragged her gaze back down to the burn line on the ground where they had put the grass fire out almost an hour ago. To her right was blackened ash. To her left was tan prairie grass.

As Cassie looked around, she saw the lights at Fort Sill's rear entrance illuminate. It must be close to 8:45 p.m., official sunset for the middle of June in Oklahoma. Fort Sill's rear entrance was perhaps three quarters of a mile away from where Cassie stood and far enough away from Fort Sill proper that none of the permanent buildings were visible. The brilliant dome of light cast by the gate lights was a startling contrast to the growing darkness of the surrounding countryside. She could see the distinctive silhouette of a canvas-covered, two-and-a-half-ton, Army M-34 class cargo truck (a deuce and a half) approaching the guard's shack in the exit lane. Odd, the truck stopped twenty feet short of the traffic barrier. Cassie watched an Army MP step out of the guard shack and walk toward the truck. A second guard stepped a couple of paces out of the guard shack to cover the first MP. The driver of the truck opened his door and stepped down. Cassie looked back up at the stars. It seemed like there were a million more.

Wait, Cassic thought, *regulations prohibit drivers from exiting a vehicle in the lane of traffic at a base entrance.* She frowned and looked back to the truck.

Vehicles were supposed to pull into the inspection parking area before the driver dismounted. There were several flashes of light as though someone was taking pictures.

Cassie's adrenalin spiked when the MP closest to the truck stiffened and fell over backward without bending at the waist. The second guard managed to turn back to the guard shack before he, too, fell to the ground. The scene didn't seem real. It was quiet. Too quiet. No gun shot reports echoed off the hills, but Cassie knew that the driver had just shot the two MPs. Cassie stood frozen for an instant.

She looked back up the burn line at the other firefighters. The wind was in her face and the other firefighters were all too far away to hear her if she called. She didn't have her cell phone on fire calls. Cassie reached for her fire radio. It hung on the collar of her fire jacket, which was hanging on the back of the firetruck at the far end of the fire line. She hung it there when the site control sergeant had declared the fire under control.

She looked back at the gate. A passenger had also gotten out of the truck. One of them must have pushed the gate release button because the traffic barrier was going up. Cassie knew that she had few options. She could run back to the other firefighters and risk losing the truck or she could go after the truck and risk not having anyone know where she had gone. She was certain of one thing. She wasn't going to let these men get away with murdering the two guards.

Cassie watched the two men return to the truck. She had been through the north gate several times during her stay here. She knew that when the truck left the gate, the driver would have to turn right, away from Cassie, and follow the access road along Deer Creek Canyon for half a mile. Then he would have to cross the Deer Creek Canyon Bridge. The access road made a 180 degree turn at the bridge. Then, the truck would come back down the other side of the canyon to within a half mile of Cassie's position. After the truck passed Cassie, the stop sign at the intersection of Highway 49 was a mere two hundred feet further on.

The truck lurched forward a few feet and stopped as if the driver lacked experience driving a stick. Cassie tensed. She had to act now; the men were leaving. Cassie felt a flash of anger.

Not on my watch!

When the truck lurched a second time, every muscle in Cassie's body exploded. She dropped everything, turned, and ran for the stop sign at the highway. She knew she couldn't make the half mile run over uneven terrain at a sprint, nor did she want to arrive at the intersection too exhausted to catch the truck. So, she ran a marathoner's pace.

There was a popular picnic area on the far side of the canyon close to the inter-section of Highway 49 and the base access road. Some civic-minded Samaritan had built a simple telephone pole bridge across the canyon for kids from the picnic area to play on. The makeshift bridge was unsteady, didn't have any handrails, and was three feet wide at its widest.

The pole bridge was Cassie's first destination. She didn't have time to descend into and climb out of the canyon. Darkness clouded the uneven ground as she ran, but when she entered a canopy of trees at the side of the canyon, she couldn't see the ground at all. She navigated by faith alone. She had about three minutes to come up with a plan.

*****

As soon as the truck was out of range of the gate's surveillance cameras, Flea reached up and turned the RF Jammer off. The MPs at headquarters would not have seen the shooting, but they would see the two dead MPs. Since the MPs were primarily concerned with keeping an intruder from breaking into the base, not someone on the base breaking out of the base, they would assume some unknown intruder or intruders had shot their way onto the base. And, while they were busy searching on base for the intruders, the three murderers would simply drive away into the night.

That was the agreed upon plan, but Flea didn't like killing people as Flat Top did. Flea looked a bit green. He wasn't accustomed to this kind of violence.

With a delighted chuckle, Flat Top asked, "Hey, Flea, you want to drive? This is your truck."

When Flea mumbled a *no*. Flat Top erupted into laughter.

*****

From inside the tree line, Cassie saw the headlights of other passing vehicles at the intersection. She kept running as she estimated the spot where the pole footbridge crossed the canyon. The brush was heavy, and the ground was a dark mystery as she ran down the steepest part of the hill at the edge of the canyon. The further she ran, the more determined she became. Adrenalin took control.

Out of the darkness, the maw of the canyon opened in front of her, and she saw the pole bridge to her right. She was close enough that she decided not to slow down.

She tried to hit the pole bridge straight on, but she didn't have the room to make a complete adjustment. Instead, she hit the bridge at a slight angle. Relying on her Marine training, she quick stepped, waved her arms, contorted her body, and willed it to stay on the poles.

She almost navigated the crossing unscathed but skidded off just short of the far side and landed knees first against the vertical, rocky side of the canyon, catapulting Cassie into a face-first slide into the gravel on the far side. Without a break in her momentum, she planted her palms on the gravel and pushed up as hard as she could. When her body came off the ground, she pumped her legs and kept running. Her face, arms, and hands were scratched, but Cassie was off the gravel and nearing the grassy picnic area before the dust settled back on the scar in the gravel.

The underbrush gave way to manicured grass as she came to the picnic area proper and began running uphill to the intersection. Uphill was no deterrent for Cassie. She often trained in hill country and found a long, uphill run easier than a long downhill run.

Cassie cleared the tree line of the picnic area and ran into the parking lot just as the truck passed in front of her. She had timed her arrival perfectly. She couldn't confront the men directly; she was unarmed and alone. Instead, she decided to get in the back of the truck and wait for an opportunity to call for reinforcements. She increased her pace to a sprint. If the driver had looked to his left, he would have seen Cassie closing on the truck from the left rear quarter. Luckily, the driver was too intent on following the dogleg in the road to the right. Cassie ran up thirty feet behind the truck. She said a quick prayer that the driver would be looking at traffic on the highway instead of in his rearview mirror. Cassie was in the open and she didn't like it.

The truck stopped at the stop sign, and Cassie ran to the drop gate. Her plan was to climb into the bed of the truck. As she approached, she saw the canvas flap tied with military efficiency down over the drop gate. She would have to reach up under the flap before she could grab the top of the drop gate.

The truck lurched as Cassie closed in, but it pulled away faster than she anticipated. She lunged for the truck, slid her hands under the canvas cover, and reached for the top of the drop gate. There was no possibility of her feet finding a hold on the bumper, so she straightened her legs to give her a little more momentum.

Her left hand missed and slipped down the drop gate's surface. Cassie's face collided with the outside of the drop gate and her body slammed into the bumper. Her feet tap-danced along the road. Cassie managed to gain a grip on the top of the drop gate with the fingertips of her right hand. She didn't fall, but she wasn't on the truck either.

Cassie simultaneously pulled with every ounce of her strength and pushed with her left hand. She jackknifed her body and reached under the canvas flap for the drop gate again. This time, she caught it with her left hand. Now, she knew she wouldn't fall. She twisted and lurched until she gained a good grip with both hands. After a breath, she threw her body away from the truck once more, trying to get her feet on the bumper, but she came up short. Her feet missed and her knees crashed into the bumper. A sharp pain seared both of her shins. Cassie felt a trickle of blood on one shin. She kept her body doubled up and tense to keep her knees on the bumper. If she relaxed for an instant, she knew they would slide off and she'd have to start again.

She made one more mighty push, drew her body into a tight fetal position, and pulled her feet toward her hands as hard as she could. Her feet landed on the bumper. With her hands and feet on the truck, Cassie dropped her torso down as far as her arms would allow and put her head between her forearms. She pushed the canvas flap away from the drop gate, slipped her head under the canvas. To her relief, the back of the truck was deserted. It was also dark. She pulled the rest of her body up and over the drop gate and into the bed of the truck.

Cassie caught a glimpse of the corner of the shipping skeleton, made of two-inch square steel tubing, before the canvas fell back into place. Military personnel secured awkward loads into skeletons for shipping. If the load were going off base, they would have put a metal covering over the whole apparatus.

Not bad for a kid who was decorating wedding cakes for a living a year ago.

She was sweating and gasping for breath. She still gripped the top lip of the drop gate with her left hand in case she had to make a hasty retreat. She turned onto her back to make herself a little more comfortable. The men weren't going to get away, but now she had to figure out what to do next. She had to find a way to contact her superiors at the Fire Training Command or the MPs at Fort Sill.

Cassie tried to look around the inside of the truck as her breathing slowed. She knew something was there, but she couldn't see what it was. She reached up and pushed the canvas cover away from the truck's drop gate.

The faintest wisp of light seeped into the back of the truck. Ice water rushed through Cassie's veins. Suspended with metal straps inside the steel shipping skeleton were two nuclear weapons, specifically, two W-63 ICBM class, thermo-nuclear weapons with a nominal yield fifty times Hiroshima. Each.

Chapter Six

Duane Connors looked at his watch. It was 8:45 p.m., and the GED class he was taking should be over by now. He had fifteen minutes to get to his night job at Happy's Quick-Mart and Bait Shop on Highway 49, north of Fort Sill. Max, the bait shop's owner, was adamant about closing the store and leaving for home at 9:00 p.m. and no later. He would close and lock Duane, who didn't have a key, inside the store. When Duane left at midnight, the door would close and lock behind him.

If class didn't run over much and his truck started, Duane could make it to the store by 9:00. The bait shop gig wasn't much of a job, more of a charity handout, but Duane didn't care. He was dedicated to doing the best job he could. He needed the money.

The instructor closed the class, "That's all for tonight, everybody. We'll see you all Wednesday. Make sure that you read chapter five of the text before next class."

Duane had three hours of restocking shelves and cleaning the bait shop. Three hours a night, every night, of minimum wage work made it possible for Duane to take this GED class. This income, combined with extra money he got from odd jobs like being a fishing and hunting guide, meant that he didn't have to borrow from his cousin to eat. After all, Duane's cousin was letting him live in a small room in his basement rent-free. The luxuries of the basement room with a small, attached bath surc beat sleeping in his car. Three months of sleeping in his back seat in El Paso introduced Duane to a life to which he never wanted to return.

While Duane lived in the room rent free, the room wasn't obligation free. In exchange for living in the basement room, Duane had to start every day with a plan for improving his life. It didn't make any difference if the plan was the same every day or if the plan changed during the day; Duane just had to have a plan and he had to do something to pursue that plan every day. He had to improve his life and work his way out of the basement.

Duane's cousin had made it clear that he was unwilling to take money away from supporting his family to help if Duane wasn't going to make every effort to pull himself out of the hole. Duane remembered the next words with laser clarity, "I won't waste my time trying to help someone who won't help himself."

The first step in Duane's current plan was to get his GED. With the certificate, he could sign up for classes at the junior college or enroll in a class at the Fire Training Center in Lawton. More education meant more opportunity for a better, higher paying job at the Army base or with the state. For now, Duane's life consisted of several goals: work hard; keep his current job; never stop applying for a better job; never stop taking classes; study; and, if time permitted, spend time with his girlfriend, Cindy.

Tonight, Duane's plan consisted of spending some leisure time with Cindy. He would drive to Cindy's parents' house on Highway 49 after work. Technically, he wouldn't spend the night, not all of it, anyway. Out of self-imposed consideration for Cindy's parents, Duane always left the house before dawn. Cindy's parents didn't require this, but they appreciated the effort. They liked Duane. Her parents believed that the relationship was solid enough for the long term and was beneficial to both.

Duane walked to the parking lot with the rest of his class (all two of them). He unlocked the door of his old green and yellow, international pickup, and stepped in. Out of habit, he checked that his broken Remington

rifle was still on the rack of the back window. This was Oklahoma, after all.

He put his key in the ignition and said
a *come-on, baby* prayer under his breath. He
turned the key, and, to his relief, the truck
turned over the first time. Duane smiled and
considered it a good omen.

He set his subconscious GPS for the
bait shop and pulled out of the community
center parking lot. It was a beautiful night:
eighty-five degrees and clear as a bell. He
liked the rush of warm air on his face and the
smell of the midsummer prairie grass behind
it.

Chapter Seven

After Cassie recovered from the sight of the nuclear weapons and started breathing again, she assessed her situation. The truck was still picking up speed. She was alone, unarmed, and had no way to communicate with her chain of command. She assumed that the men would drive as far from the base as they could as fast as they could, but the driver might stop or pull over at any moment. Cassie had to be ready to bail out and she needed a plan. Her first objective was to not let the men catch her unless it gave her a re-markable advantage. These men had already demonstrated that they were willing to kill military personnel, and she had no illusions that they would hesitate to kill a lone, female Marine. These men could make Cassie disap-pear. Second, she couldn't allow them to get away with these nuclear weapons. If she had to, Cassie would let the men get away to maintain her contact with the weapons. Fi-nally, if she accomplished the first two objec-tives, she would bring these men to justice for the murders of the two MPs and for acts of terrorism.

Cassie decided that when the truck slowed, she would roll out of the back and determine why they were slowing. She didn't want to jump off the truck if the driver was just turning a corner because she might not be able to get on again. She also didn't want to wait on the truck too long and risk being seen jumping from the truck. For now, all Cassie could do was ride in the back of the truck, stay alert, and keep track of the men and the nukes. She focused on noticing when the truck might be slowing down. When the opportunity arose, she would contact Fort Sill.

*****

Fifteen months ago, Cassie would never have believed that she'd be tracking terrorists and stolen nuclear weapons across the Oklahoma hill country. Fifteen months ago, Cassie was a second shift manager at a Parris, California bakery that specialized in wedding cakes. While Cassie was a natural manager, the bakery owner valued her most for her artistic eye. Cassie had a knack for decorating wedding cakes. She made roses out of icing that looked so real a person could almost smell them. Everyone who knew Cassie or had seen one of her creations agreed that she had a promising career as a confectioner and that before long, she would own her own business and have a reputation throughout Southern California.

But, for Cassie, there was something missing. She considered her future as a local business owner and wasn't excited. It was mundane and uninspired--a slow, boring rut. Cassie had excelled in high school and earned admission to a local college, but in her first year, college lost its appeal as well. She knew that her family expected her to complete college, but she also knew that college was unsatisfying. She wanted something bigger than herself. She wanted to spend her life making a difference in the world.

At times, Cassie considered the Peace Corps, becoming a civilian firefighter, or becoming a police officer. The prospects were exciting, but to excel over her competition, she needed some experience. Cassie had many long conversations with her close confidant, her Aunt Lenell. Aunt Lenell understood Cassie's quandary and sympathized with her sense of being rudderless. Aunt Lenell acknowledged that Cassie must leave and pursue her own life. She also emphasized with Cassie that she might want to return to her life and family in SoCal someday.

During one conversation, Cassie said, "It feels like a nagging itch that I must scratch before it consumes me."

Aunt Lenell reflected Cassie's message. "I understand. You need to go find yourself, find where you fit into the world, see if you measure up, and test yourself. I always knew that you'd leave someday. It sounds to me like your primary question is, 'Which way do I go?'"

"That's it exactly!" Cassie exclaimed. "I want to test myself out in the world and see what I'm made of. I want to see the world, experience the people, and to be part of something bigger than myself, something that has real meaning."

"When you do go, we'll be here for you--a base of operations, so to speak. When you need to leave, leave. We'll understand, but you must stay in touch. We still need you in our lives. You're always welcome to come back if that's where life takes you."

There was one other notion that came up whenever Cassie contemplated her future. The Sing family had a strong military tradition. Cassie's grandfather, father, and uncle had all served in the U.S. Army. Two other uncles had served in the U.S. Navy. A female cousin was attending the Air Force Academy, and a male cousin was an infantryman in the U.S. Marines. The Sing family believed it was their duty to spend some part of their life serving their country and protecting the rights and freedoms they all enjoyed as Americans. Great-Grandpa Sing endorsed this notion as soon as he emigrated from India. While the military tradition didn't formally extend to the young women of the family, the elders expected every family member to serve, to volunteer, or contribute in some way.

Cassie had several conversations with her father and Uncle Brian about joining the military. She also interviewed recruiters of the four branches at the recruiting station in San Diego. Still, she wasn't ready to make the commitment. It wasn't that she was unsure of herself or her abilities, it just seemed that she hadn't given the decision enough time and consideration to be sure that it was the right path for her. After all, entering the military was a life-changing decision. Cassie *was* sure of one thing beyond any shadow of doubt: if she went into the military, she wanted to be *in* the military. She wanted to experience all the action the lifestyle offered. She was on the cusp of a decision to enlist when she had the dream.

Chapter Eight

When the dream opened, the sky was mint green. Cassie didn't know why her dreams always opened with the sky the color of a green mint, but they did. As soon as Cassie realized she was dreaming, she changed the color of the sky to blue. She wondered many times why the part of her mind that created her dreams insisted on a mint green sky. As a child, Cassie found that she could change or direct any portion of the dream she wanted or just go with the flow of the dream as it unfolded. Her dreams were always entertaining and interesting.

The air around her was hot, muggy, and stone still. The jungle seemed normal enough: green, brown, and cloaked in sha-dows. She looked down and the dirt was brown and moss-covered. The color of the sky as the dream started was the one obvious break from reality. The leaves of the jungle plants that brushed her skin as she walked down the path were cool and comforting. The first surprise of her dream was that her feet were the size of a small child's. She was star-tled but calmed herself in a single heartbeat. Sometimes, too much of a reaction in a dream snapped her awake. Right now, she didn't want to wake up. She wanted to see where this dream was going to take her.

Cassie saw dozens of other six-to-eight-year-old children walking in the same direction on parallel paths. She couldn't see anyone older or younger. All the children were going in the same downhill direction. Cassie looked above and beyond the jungle whenever she could. A jungle-covered mountain was behind her. Everyone must have come from the mountain. In the distance before her, Cassie saw the ocean. The ocean seemed to be their destination. For now, Cassie just kept walking.

She noticed that she wasn't hungry or thirsty. She didn't feel threatened. After a few seconds of walking, she noticed that the other children had aged. They now seemed to be twelve or thirteen. When she looked at her own hands, it was obvious that she had also aged. The further down the path they walked, the older they got. Her intuition told her that no one could turn around and walk back up the path.

Presently, she came to an open, grassy area and followed the crowd to the crest of a hill. From her vantage point, she looked behind her and saw that they were on an island with a white-capped mountain in the middle. The ocean was visible in every direction. She saw other grassy breaks in the jungle she and the teenagers had walked across in their march toward the sea.

The flowing force of the dream urged her to keep walking. She watched the age of the people around her progress as they walked. They talked and laughed amongst themselves, though she couldn't hear them. She could see that they were talking. Cassie had never developed the sense of hearing in her dreams. If someone talked to her in her dream, it was still silent, but somehow Cassie knew what he or she was saying as if she knew the script beforehand and was matching the words to the movement of their lips. In this dream, she didn't have anyone close enough to talk to, so she just kept walking.

Not long after passing the opening in the jungle, the air was cooler, and she could smell the salty tang of the ocean. She knew she must be getting close to the beach. She looked at the people around her. They were all adults. She didn't have to look at her hands to know that she, too, was an adult.

There were adult men and women all over the beach, but it didn't feel crowded. It was obvious who the newcomers were. They milled around looking lost. Many of the people who had been on the beach for a while seemed to be content to lie around, sleep, work on their suntans, or swim and wade in the shallow water. Others built shelters and amenities like chairs and hammocks. Some of these structures were quite sophisticated, and there were even a few elaborate tree houses. The one thing that Cassie knew was that no one could ever go back into the jungle or to the mountain.

On the horizon, there was a jumble of dark, churning clouds. Lightning coursed back and forth with brilliant flashes of color. Occasionally, Cassie could feel the concussive impact of the thunder, but there was no sound accompanying the storm. The display was intimidating. Those who ventured into the water stayed close to the beach where it was quiet and secure. The beach felt like home. The beach would protect them. The beach had everything any of them could want. Someone had even gathered food and water at various spots on the beach. Why would anyone want to leave the security and familiarity of the beach?

Every so often, however, someone tried to swim away from the beach toward the storms on the horizon. The sea would rise and try to scare them back to the beach. Waves grew higher, winds got stronger, whitecaps formed, and the salt spray stung their skin. From the safety of the beach, people could see the sea turn darker as seaweed grew thick and tangled around the swimmers' feet. Sea animals brushed the swimmers' bodies and tentacles trapped their arms. Leaving the beach was a frightening endeavor. Some of the bravest tried to leave the beach several times, learning from their previous attempts.

Over time, a small percentage of the swimmers were able to swim away from the beach and overcome their fears and the threats of the intimidating sea. They never returned. The rest of the population noticed the successful and unsuccessful swimmers but remained entrenched in their lives on the beach. They lived normal lives filled with families and careers. They became the pillars of their society.

After what Cassie perceived to be a couple of days on the beach, she found herself standing at the water's edge, staring at the churning clouds in the distance. She had no choice; the dream brought her here. She walked into the sea, and the sea rose to push her back. The winds grew stronger, and the

water got colder. Cassie didn't change anything; she just went with the flow. When the
water got knee deep, she swung her arms to
keep her balance. She could taste the salt in
the air. The sky overhead grew darker. She
used her hands to paddle the water at her
sides. The water became waist deep, then
chest deep. The waves and the wind raged
higher and higher around her, but the passage
didn't seem any more difficult. As the waves
rose, her ability to wade in the surf grew
stronger. She looked away whenever the
wind blew salt water in her face. As everything around her became more intimidating,
she found more strength and a deeper determination to keep moving ahead. She was
driving herself. She knew the people on the
beach were watching her. She knew that they
were thinking about how difficult it must be
getting for her. They didn't know that her
ability to cope with the turmoil around her
was growing faster than the turmoil itself.
She had no fear. It was getting easier, not
harder, for Cassie to keep going. She wanted
to test herself against the storms that were
getting closer and more violent.

Cassie soon found that her hands and
feet were warmer and not numb and frozen.
From her vantage point in the water, the

waves looked as tall as buildings, but she was comfortable using the motion of the waves to propel herself forward. The winds were her ally now and helped her know her course in the sea. She could no longer see the island, the flashes of lightning on the horizon, or even the sky overhead. It didn't bother Cassie that everything but the little circle of water around her was in chaos.

There was something else, though, something a hair's breadth beyond her reach. She couldn't see it or feel it, but it was there. She needed to see what it was. She passed an imaginary hand across the horizon, or what she thought was the horizon, palm down as though brushing aside a curtain. Almost immediately, the seas calmed, and the winds abated. The sea sprays fell back into the sea. The blue sky broke through the clouds. Cassie still couldn't identify the sensation, but it was stronger.

Cassie shook her head to remove the water from her face and the remaining veils from her mind. She reached out and scanned for the sensation again, and there it was: a sound in the distance. For the first time in her life, Cassie could hear a sound in her dreams. It took a second to get loud enough for her to realize that she was hearing music. The music was a jumble, but it was music played by horns.

As Cassie listened, the music grew louder and more strident. The horns didn't have the clarity of tone that was characteristic of French horns or the patriotic call of bugles. There were horns of all types that seemed to be trying to outplay all the others. The horns were a bit off key from one another and a little off tempo from the group. They sounded more like a gaggle of bagpipes than the horns of a symphony. The horns grew louder and more cacophonous with every passing second. Cassie now understood why bagpipes could instill terror in an enemy before a battle. The horns felt like an assault.

Through it all, though, Cassie recognized the song. It was The Marine's Hymn. As she listened, the hymn became more coherent, more melodious. Cassie was drawn to the emotion of the hymn. It seemed right to her, almost comforting as it raised images of tradition in her mind. The hymn was bigger than Cassie, and she wanted to be a part of it. Out of respect, Cassie stayed still in the water until the hymn ended. She was alone in a calm sea beneath a blue sky, and the stormy horizon was now clear.

She waited for the dream to continue but it didn't. Cassie drifted for a brief instant and then decided that the dream was over. She could take over and direct the dream if she wanted, but the message was complete. Her two options were to go back to a dreamless sleep or wake up. She mentally blinked. When she closed her mind's eyes, she was dreaming. When she opened her real eyes, she was awake.

Cassie lay still and stared at her bedroom ceiling replaying the dream to help her solidify the memory. She turned on her nightlight and reached for her dream diary. Cassie had recorded her dreams for as long as she could remember. It was an interesting pastime, but she didn't know how much credibility, if any, she'd assigned to the hobby. Most of the time, keeping the diary seemed no more significant than bird watching.

Cassie struggled with what to write. She didn't know if the dream was echoing a decision that she had already made, or if she had finalized the decision based on the dream. She didn't know and she didn't care. She'd made her decision.

She enjoyed the experience of advanced dream states. Being able to manipulate her dreams while dreaming opened a whole world of recreational possibilities. She could fly, swim under water without an air supply, or go anywhere she wished. She opened her dream diary and found four blank pages. If she was concise, this dream would fill the book. Finishing a dream book always filled Cassie with a sense of accomplishment.

After she completed the dream transcript, she put her diary and all thoughts of the dream aside. She had too many other things on her mind this morning. Even though it was a little after 3:00 a.m., Cassie knew she wasn't going to get back to sleep. She wasn't one to just lounge in bed after waking up, so she headed for the shower. As she waited for the water to get hot, she wondered for the hundredth time if she would ever understand the significance or the symbolism of the mint green sky.

Chapter Nine

The military police guard at Fort Sill's north gate didn't make the required 9:00 p.m. com check with the duty sergeant. He tried to call the gate, but no one answered. When the duty sergeant switched to the live feed of the north gate, he saw the feet of an MP lying on the ground next to the guard shack and called the duty officer.

After one glance at the screen, the duty officer shouted, "I'm declaring a Lockdown Alpha."

The duty sergeant picked up an emergency procedures manual, opened it to the Lockdown Alpha tab, and started making calls.

The duty officer picked up the public-address microphone and said, "Scramble Alpha, Scramble Alpha."

By the time the duty officer trotted to the jeeps outside, five armed MPs and a field medic were waiting for him.

"North gate, MP down. Go!" he barked and jumped into the jeep.

As the duty sergeant made the listed calls, MPs closed all access points on Fort Sill and raised all permanent barriers on base access and egress roads. The duty sergeant dispatched extra MPs armed with assault rifles to all base gates. He called the nuclear weapons maintenance and nuclear weapons storage after-hours phone numbers and ordered a complete inventory, focusing on recent shipments. The occupants of the base's major buildings locked their respective buildings down, including the post PX, Commissary, Officers' Club, the NCO Club, post bowling alley, and the post theater. Traffic lights all over the base went red in both directions. The MP recon center launched search drones to supplement perimeter fence patrols, and a dozen drone pilots dispatched tactical drones over the interior grounds. They searched for anything out of the ordinary.

Fort Sill was officially locked down.

*****

At 9:07 p.m., the three Army jeeps stopped a few yards short of Fort Sill's north gate. The MP duty officer and several members of the military police jumped out of the jeeps and formed a defensive arc facing the guard shack and the downed MPs. Two of the MPs ran, with rifles in the firing position, across the open space to the first downed man. The sergeant checked for a pulse and then looked back to the duty officer and shook his head. Two other MPs kept their rifles trained on the guard shack as they checked the other downed guard and confirmed that he was dead as well.

One MP kneeling at the second dead man reported to the duty officer, "Fifteen minutes, half hour at the most, Sir."

"Roger that."

On the outside, the officer was the picture of military efficiency. On the inside, his rage was drowned by overwhelming sorrow. The combat-hardened officer served two tours and had lost men in Iraq. It never got easier, and memories flooded back.

Two MPs entered the guard shack and verified that it was empty. There was nowhere else for an assailant to hide. The site was secure.

"All clear," the lead MP shouted.

Two other MPs checked the open ground beyond the shack and echoed the all-clear.

"Get the medics and an ambulance up here. Davis, raise the hard barricades." The MP duty officer ordered, "Move your perimeter ten yards beyond the guard shack. Dispatch a jeep and two guards to the outer limit of the access road. I'm closing this gate until further notice."

Two MPs drove their jeep out Deer Creek Canyon Road to the leading edge of the park a few hundred feet off Highway 49. Anyone could turn off the highway and access the picnic park, but not the access road.

Local radio stations reported that the military had closed Fort Sill until further notice. For most of the morning commuter traffic, the detour around Fort Sill to the east gate wasn't a major inconvenience. The inbound commuter traffic would hold at the east gate until the base reopened. Their managers would overlook reasonable tardiness this morning.

"Kinsey, download a copy of the security tapes for the last hour to the guard shack video system. I want to review them immediately."

The duty officer stepped over to where the medic was examining one of the fallen MP's. The medic reported, "Gun shots, close range, small caliber, maybe fifteen, twenty minutes ago."

The duty officer keyed his walkie-talkie, "Sir, gun shot, twenty-minute perimeter."

Kinsey called from the guard shack, "Sir, tape's up. A deuce and a half exited the base through the gate just after the MPs went down. The number was covered, and the three occupants shielded their faces. We don't have cameras at the highway. I don't know if they went east or west."

"Good work, Kinsey. Hold the tape. I want to see it. Contact the motor pool. Tell them the situation. Have them search for and account for all deuces."

The duty officer turned back to his cell phone and said, "We have three suspects. They exited, I repeat 'exited,' Fort Sill via the north gate a few minutes before 9:00 p.m. They were in a deuce and a half. The identification number was covered. We don't know if they went east or west. Yes, sir, another hour. If we don't have any incidents on base, I'll clear the lock-down."

Next, the duty officer speed dialed the Oklahoma State Police Liaison Officer. Normally, the duty officer's jurisdiction ended at the gate, but two of his MPs had been murdered, and the evidence showed that the suspects had fled into the Oklahoma countryside.

The duty officer explained the facts to the State Police Liaison Officer, then added, "They are armed and have already killed two of our MPs. Yes. Thank you. Stop the truck and detain the occupants until we arrive. I'm dispatching jeeps east and west and, with your permission, I'm calling in the Army Air Cavalry. They can have helicopters in the air in ten minutes. When we find them, I want them held so tight that the driver can't see out his windshield."

"Sir, the motor pool reports that the transponder on M34-TMU-151 isn't transmitting."

The duty officer nodded and turned back to his cell phone, "We have evidence that the truck's designation is M34-TMU-151. Keep me apprised. I'll let you know if we have any new information."

Another Army ambulance and an Army jeep with four MPs in it pulled up as the duty officer was closing his phone. He pointed to the driver of the jeep and said, "Take two men and go east on 49." He pointed to the driver of one of the other jeeps and said, "Take two men and go west on 49." To both drivers, he said, "We're trying to locate deuce and a half designation M34-TMU-151. The occupants killed two MPs. If you locate the truck, call it in. Don't approach M34-TMU-151 except to save lives. This is an authorized joint operation with the state police. Go."

The duty officer flipped his phone open and speed dialed the Army Air Cavalry duty desk.

Again, he explained the situation, "I'm requesting two Black Hawks be placed on crew ready, hot stand-by. I want a full hostage recovery team in both. I will radio you when we have a destination."

It was going to be a long night.

Chapter Ten

The deuce slowed down. It had been about forty-five minutes since she had dropped into the back of the truck. A quick calculation told Cassie that they were fifteen to twenty-five miles west or northwest of Fort Sill's back gate on Highway 49. They might be on State Route 58 or State Route 115 if the driver was able to turn onto the intersecting highway without Cassie noticing. She couldn't see outside the truck but was sure that they hadn't turned off Highway 49. It had to be close to 9:30 p.m.

Cassie rolled onto but not over the drop gate until her feet touched the truck bumper. She lowered her body until her head and shoulders were below the canvas back flap, and stole a quick glance right and left, careful not to allow her head to show beyond the side of the truck. Except for the stars, there were no lights visible at all, even in the distance. There were no buildings, no signs of improvements, and no refined road other than Highway 49. The truck was turning onto a private gravel driveway. Cassie looked down at the ground. In the glow of the tail-lights, the gravel was rutted and irregular. The owner hadn't graded the driveway in a long time. The original red sand showed through the gravel in more places than not. Cassie saw several sets of tire tracks: one looked big enough to be from a tractor-trailer rig.

The dirt road was rough and hilly, but the turns were long enough to accommodate larger trucks. The wash made it uncomfortable to navigate at more than ten mph. Cassie did the math: a mile every six minutes. She guessed that their destination was close, so she endured the bone-jarring ride and stayed on the back of the truck. When the truck turned one way or the other to follow a curve in the road, Cassie slid to the side of the turn. This allowed her to see a sliver of the road in front of the truck for a moment. She could see the layout of the surrounding area just enough to reassure herself that they weren't too close to the end of the road.

Less than five minutes had passed when the truck slowed and started a gentle turn to the right. When Cassie pulled herself to the right side and peeked around the edge of the truck. She saw a distinct glow of artificial lighting over the next hillcrest. If the truck turned right into a lighted area, she had to be ready to run into the desert and disappear before anyone noticed her. Cassie tensed.

*****

At 9:20 p.m., Captain Simeon Palmer, Commanding Officer of the Nuclear Sciences Training Command at Fort Sill was relaxing in his apartment at the bachelor officers' quarters when his phone rang.

Simeon's cell phone rang with the ring tone that he had selected for business calls. "Captain Palmer!"

"Sir, this is Sergeant Foster. One of our students, Lance Corporal Cassandra Sing, went missing this evening while assisting our local fire crews on a small grass fire north of the base. The fire line supervisor first noticed that she was missing at twenty forty-five hours."

"UA?"

"I have no evidence of that, Sir. My first guess is no. She is an exemplary student, always involved, and second in her class. Right now, she is just missing without explanation. The fire line supervisor has dispatched teams of firefighters to walk the fire line and search for Lance Corporal Sing. We have requested that a drone be dispatched to the area to conduct a wider search."

"Well done, Foster. Keep me apprised of any new developments. I'll call it in to the MP Duty Desk."

Captain Palmer ended the call and speed dialed the MP Duty Desk.

*****

The deuce and a half made its final right turn into the lighted area, and Cassie launched herself off the truck to the left and ran toward the nearest brush. She stayed hunched over with her arms up around her head to break her profile. When she reached the brush, she stopped and crouched down without raising any more dust than necessary. A dust cloud would reflect the light from the parking area. She also picked up the first bit of debris that she could find and held it in front of her face to break up her human profile. Once she was as invisible as she could make herself, she froze. Motion of any kind might also catch the attention of anyone looking in her direction. Once Cassie was stone still and her profile obscured, she was just part of the grassland background.

*****

Duane drove into the empty parking lot of Happy's Quick-Mart. The parking lot lights went out and a second later, most of the interior lights went out as well. The one source of light in the area was the security lights on the expansive, covered front porch. Tree-branch chairs and rough log posts and railings gave the place an old west look that Duane liked. Duane tapped on the window to get Max's attention.

Max let Duane in with, "'Bout time you got here. Men's room needs a little extra cleaning, and someone spilled a soda by the ice machines. There's some leftover chili if you want it."

Without waiting for a response, Max headed for the door.

"Good night, Max," Duane called.

Max waved back over his shoulder but didn't turn around or say anything else. He had the season finale of his favorite dance show recorded on his DVR. He just knew that the baseball player and his professional partner were going to win. They were both so athletic and graceful.

As Max left the parking lot, Duane let the self-locking door close. For the next three hours, Duane was alone. The first thing he did, as usual, was clean and disinfect an end section of the snack counter and spread his homework out. Duane worked hard at the bait shop, but he also took some time each evening to review and catch up on his homework. He scheduled a guided horseback tour into Diamond Back Canyon for the next morning. He needed the money.

Even after spending some of his shift doing homework, Duane accomplished more in a shift than any of Max's previous night managers. Duane was a whirlwind of efficiency when he was working. He swept and mopped floors, cleaned and stocked shelves, washed and refilled salt and peppershakers, and emptied the grills' grease traps. The last chore that he did before he left at midnight was to clean and restock the bathrooms. Usually, he reviewed his schoolwork as he worked. With his books open, he could review or check any confusion he had with his studies. Between his custodial labors and the review of his studies, the three hours at the bait shop flew by.

Tonight was different. Duane was going to see Cindy tonight, and thoughts of Cindy trumped any efforts to concentrate on his homework. She was the biggest bright spot in his life. He liked imagining his future with Cindy. Thoughts of his future with Cindy morphed into recalling the past few years.

Duane's father was an unskilled, itinerant laborer. Duane and his mother followed Duane's dad to whatever potential menial job was next on the horizon: farm labor, the oil industry, or housing construction. Duane had never completed a full year of school in one location, and the family seldom received mail that the post office hadn't forwarded from somewhere else.

At the time, Duane didn't know if either of his parents had any brothers or sisters. Duane didn't. The three of them lived a nomadic life with few friends and no known relatives. They lived a hand-to-mouth life on the edge of the lowest level of the middle class. But Duane's parents were good people. On rare occasion, the family accepted food from local food banks, but they never accepted welfare. Duane's mother worked hard to keep the family on the positive side of abject poverty.

In the middle of Duane's junior year of high school, his father had, once again, worked a temporary job to completion. There were no more trees to prune, and his dad didn't know how to drive the big bug spray units. The family was moving on. Duane would lose his first chance to be in school at the end of a school year. He already owned his books for the year, so his mother was going to tutor Duane through the last of the year's studies.

Duane's mother and father had dropped Duane off at the high school and drove out to the pecan orchards his father worked to get his last paycheck. Duane had closed out his accounts at the school library and cafeteria. He had a closing interview with his counselor and collected his records. Duane then walked out the front door of the school and dropped his paperwork on the bus stop bench to wait for his parents. They had already given up the efficiency apartment and lost their deposit. Everything the family owned was in their car.

Duane waited and waited at the bus stop for his parents. By dusk, it was apparent that his parents weren't coming. It would be two days before Duane would find out that his parents died in a head-on crash with a farm truck. That afternoon was the start of three horrible years of hunger and homelessness.

*****

Flea was lost in thought as the truck made the final turn into the open parking area in front of the hunting cabin. He once again thanked his good fortune for meeting the two leaders (The Major and Flat Top) of the local chapter of the Americans for Constitutional Reform (ACR) a few months ago. Flea was still in the Army but knew that he'd soon re-ceive a grudgingly issued honorable dis-charge. Flea and the Army (or any form of authority) didn't get along. He was angry, willful, resentful, and deceitful. He believed that, if he could get away with it, it was okay to break the rules. Laws were an artifact of life designed to keep other people out of his way. The Army had taken him off the streets and provided a positive direction for his floundering life, but the situation had dege-nerated. The Army wanted Flea out, and Flea wanted out of the Army.

Flea considered the day he first be-came associated with the ACR to be the first day of his true life. Everything before that day was a nightmare that he wanted to forget. Everything after that day was real and ful-filling. The ACR and its members became Flea's family. He was becoming somebody important. He had a bright future.

Flea was playing pool in the barracks day room with other enlisted men. The day room was stark and depressing. It had a fifty-year-old, green asbestos tile floor, walls that were painted grey once a year, a late model television set (off limits until 6:00 p.m. on a workday), a couple of old couches, a pool table, and a closet full of unused books, games, and puzzles. Flea had snuck away from his menial job at the weapons maintenance facility. The workers at the facility never noticed the janitor, much less if the janitor was missing.

One of the men playing pool and two observers were attempting to sing harmony along with the latest rap hit on the radio. They were convinced that they were beyond wonderful. The singers imagined themselves to be the next greatest musical prodigies to grace the rap industry. They were more than willing to let the Army take care of them until the music-loving population discovered them. They were willing to play pool, sing, and drift through a pointless Army career forever if that's what it took.

One of the singers was playing pool with a soldier who saw himself as a pool shark. Another wannabe pool shark stood nearby, watching and waiting for his turn at the mark. Both just knew that they would be pool-hustling celebrities someday. Today, they were playing for a quarter a game. Day Room rules forbade gambling because people cheated, and fights were inevitable. The players understood, without words, that all bets must be settled by the end of the day. None of the players were any good at pool, so no one made any significant money any-way.

Of course, Flea was, as always, enga-ged in his favorite pastime: complaining. Flea could describe what was wrong with the government, the Army, and the officers ap-pointed above him. He could debunk the lies on the evening news, in his marriage, and just about every other aspect of his life that he perceived as wrong. Complaining was the activity that Flea most enjoyed and the one activity he was good at. He didn't realize that if he had applied just one tenth of his grin-ching energy to his Army job performance, he would've been a reasonably successful bottom-basement variety private.

That day, Flea was playing pool and complaining about why the Army Promotion Board didn't promote him during the last ad-vancement cycle. Of course, no one was lis-tening. Everyone else was lost in his own fantasies. Everyone, that is, except Dennis. Dennis was deciding if Flea was malcontent enough to join the little militia group that Dennis supported. Flea cycled in and out of the game for the next hour. In the end, he was all complained out, had broken even, and decided to head home.

"Hey, hold up a sec," Dennis said as Flea walked by. "I'll walk with you. My name's Dennis. I was listening to what you were saying in there. It sounded good, a little rough around the edges, maybe, but it all seemed right on point. You're Wajowski, aren't you? Everybody calls you Flea?"

Without slowing his pace, Flea said, "Yeah, so? You want something?"

"Actually, yes. I want to be associated with clear-thinking adults, like you, who aren't afraid to speak out about this nation's wrongs and evils. I believe in much of what you're saying. America could be so much more than it is. There're a lot of us who agree with you and think that we should do something to even the playing field a little, to bring America back to clear thinking. Right now, people who share our vision are forming small groups all over the country, and we're getting stronger. I think you'd be a good fit and might be a significant player when the time comes."

"Sounds like a white supremacist group. Not interested." Flea didn't look at Dennis and kept walking.

"Yep, it does sound that way, but we aren't white supremacists. The logic and deductions of those groups is flawed, limited, and designed to recruit new followers. We want to restructure our government back to the original design in the Constitution, back to what the writers of the Constitution wanted to give to all Americans. We want the same reforms in our government that you were saying you wanted. The American Dream isn't dead; it's just buried under bureaucratic BS."

Flea stopped. "I'm not much of a joiner."

"Good! There is nothing to join. We invite selected speakers to address a general audience. And then discuss what they said. No one will tell you what to think, how to act, what to say. Every now again, a few people with the right potential are invited to join an inner core group. No obligation. You've got nothing to lose and everything to gain. If you don't agree with the message, quit coming, no strings. If nothing else, there's free coffee and doughnuts." Dennis paused a moment and gauged the reaction on Flea's face.

Flea didn't have any plans for Saturday night. His wife would be working. If the speaker was too lame, he'd just leave. Flea shrugged, "What the hell?"

"Great, the meeting starts at 7 p.m. in the rec room at the Lake Terrace Apartments. See you there?"

"Yeah, we'll see, maybe. I gotta go."

"We want to return to a strong government and a strong military where educated, adult males like you and I have a chance to get a piece of the American Dream." Dennis watched Flea's reaction. Flea nodded and almost imperceptivity nodded in the affirmative. Good, Dennis had set the hook.

Flea searched Dennis's face as if Dennis might admit he was deceiving him. Dennis didn't blink, twitch, or sweat. He kept an even smile. Maybe this guy was on the up-and-up. Flea could imagine that a country that had returned to the original intent of the Constitution might benefit him. He decided to go to just this one meeting.

Chapter Eleven

Cassie sat motionless on the side of the driveway, concealed by the low brush. An instant memory flooded her consciousness as she waited for the world around her to move forward. She remembered how it felt to sit frozen on a bus at the Paris Island Reception Center, head bowed, hands on her knees, waiting for the drill instructors to scream at her again. A female drill instructor had come on the bus and told the recruits how to assume the correct position of respect: both feet on the floor, head bowed, hands on your knees or holding your personal items. She emphasized the requirement for complete silence. Then, she stepped off the bus and the door closed.

After a few minutes of silence, the bus door hissed open again. Drill Instructor Peters (not Drill Sergeant Peters, but Drill *Instructor* Peters) stepped aboard. She was dressed in khaki and creased from head to toe with military precision. She had an intimidating array of stripes, cords, medals, and sashes. She was recruiting poster perfection from her hair and uniform to her degree of fitness. As soon as Drill Instructor Peters had both feet on the main bus landing, she zeroed in on one of the recruits and started yelling.

"Who told you to look at me? The drill instructor ordered you to keep your head bowed. Can you not follow orders?" Drill Instructor Peter's face was brushing the recruit's hair.

The original drill instructor jumped to the aid of Drill Instructor Peters and shouted, "Are we going to have a problem, recruit? Are you going to follow orders or am I going to have to wash you out?"

The two screaming drill instructors were relentless for thirty seconds. The pale girl was chagrined but not shaking from having the drill instructor single her out so soon. The girl was, however, able to continue an endless barrage of answers.

"Yes, Drill Instructor. No, Drill Instructor. Yes, Drill Instructor."

Drill Instructor Peters lowered her voice to a venomous whisper, "I'm going to be watching you, recruit. Don't make me repeat myself. Understand?"

"Yes, Drill Instructor," the girl shouted.

The girl didn't know that the cadre of drill instructors allowed few recruits to get through the first week of basic training without a tongue-lashing for some infraction or another. Almost all the young women came away from the first forty-eight hours of Marine Recruit Training feeling as though they personified the most incompetent, screwed-up Marine volunteer whoever entered the Paris Island Reception Center.

Drill Instructor Peters shouted a string of instructions. "When I give the order to fall in, you will exit the bus as fast as possible. Fall in on the yellow footprints next to the bus. Start at the front of the formation and work back with no open footprints in the middle of the formation. There will be no discussion, no questions, and no noise. You will stand still. You will place personal items across your chest with your arms folded across the personal items. Otherwise, your arms will be at your sides with your hands closed around your thumbs. Do not look to your left or to your right. I repeat, you will be silent. Do you understand?"

The recruits answered as one in the loudest voices they could muster, "Yes, Drill Instructor."

Drill Instructor Peters looked at her associate with mock horror, "Drill Instructor Mathews, is this cheerleader camp or Marine Corps Recruit Training?"

It was a rhetorical question. Drill Instructor Mathews didn't answer. She also didn't smile.

Drill Instructor Peters shouted, "This is the Marine Corps Recruit Training Detachment, Paris Island, South Carolina, not cheerleader camp. The next time I ask a question, people sleeping in Charleston better hear your answer. Do you understand me?"

The recruits tried to increase the volume of their collective answer. "Yes, Drill Instructor!"

"Better. Again! Do you understand me?"

"Yes, Drill Instructor!"

"Better. Again, do you understand me?"

"Yes, Drill Instructor!"

The two drill instructors exited the bus and a silent pall fell over the bus. Seconds seemed like hours. The women were nervous and touchy. They seemed ready to explode off the bus when the drill instructor gave the order. The order didn't come. The rate of breathing slowed on the bus. They collectively relaxed and fidgeted at the same time.

"Fall in!"

Cassie jumped as much as the others did. She stood up, determined to stay as close to the girl in front of her as possible. Cassie was surprised at how fast everyone got off the bus. A few steps later, she stood on her yellow footprints, one step behind the girl in front of her. She put her hands at her side, stood at attention, took a deep breath, and closed her eyes to collect her thoughts. The drill instructor was at her side in an instant, screaming into Cassie's ear. In a heartbeat, two more drill instructors surrounded Cassie.

"Did I not make myself clear? I said to fall in with no gaps in the ranks! Are you awake? Do you want to run home to mama?" The drill instructor screamed everything at least two, sometimes three or four times.

Cassie looked down in amazement. Her attention had drifted. While Cassie's eyes were closed, her attention had drifted, and the girl in front of her stepped forward to fill an empty set of footprints. That left the yellow footprints in front of Cassie empty. *Shit, shit, shit!*

"Yes, Drill Instructor. No, Drill Instructor!"

The drill instructors moved away. None of the other recruits looked at Cassie.

"Listen up! This recruit screwed up! That means that everybody does it again! And you'll keep doing it until everyone falls out like Marines! Next time, do it silently! You made enough noise last time to wake up half the base! I get a call about the noise from the base commander and I'm going to be pissed! Next time, you will fall in faster! I don't like it when slow, lazy recruits keep me waiting! Get back on the bus!"

As one, the drill instructors started screaming, "Move, move, move!"

The recruits hadn't gotten seated when Drill Instructor Peters yelled, "Fall in!"

The second time, Cassie fell out like a Marine recruit. She vowed to never lose focus again. The women re-boarded the bus and fell out four times. All was silent after the last maneuver. All were finally in proper ranks. The scene was surreal, like something from a movie.

"I'm going to call your names. You will answer, 'Here, Drill Instructor,' and then step up to this door. A drill instructor will direct you to a phone. You will call home and tell your family that you arrived safely at Paris Island. The phone calls will be short. This isn't a social call. After your call, you will follow the yellow line to the next station. Do you understand?"

"Yes, Drill Instructor!"

A Marine private stood beside the open door. She wasn't a drill instructor; she wore a standard issued eight-point field cap, not the distinctive drill sergeants "Smokey Bear" hat. The private was waiting for a sign to begin. After receiving the cue, the private called names.

"Smith, Linda; Hernandez, Malinda; Schneider, Doris…"

Every now and then, she would pause and wait for an event inside before calling the next name. Cassie was supposed to look straight ahead, but she couldn't help noticing the women around her and the variety of names called. Each of the ninety-six recruits was different. Cassie knew that the Marines preached and practiced teamwork, but these people were all so different from each other. They represented every race and ethnic background, including some that Cassie didn't recognize. They were from all major religions and two dozen countries of origin. All spoke English, at least to some degree, but many spoke other languages as well. Some came from money. Some came from poverty. Several were tenth-generation

Americans, and others were working for their citizenship in conjunction with their service in the Marines. The differences seemed end-less. Cassie wondered how she was ever going to connect with anyone in such a diverse group to form the sisterhood she had heard about so often.

The clerk had called more than half of the recruits before she called, "Sing, Cassandra."

Cassie walked into a room about the size of a high school classroom. It was devoid of furnishings or decoration, and the cinder block walls were painted grey. Ugly, green tile covered the floor. A dozen phones were mounted along one wall. There were no considerations for comfort. A girl stood at each of the phones but one. A drill instructor stood by the open phone with an unspoken gesture to Cassie.

As Cassie stepped up to the wall, the drill instructor said, "Make it quick. You have a long night ahead of you."

Cassie punched in her home number. As the phone rang, Cassie saw two drill instructors step up alongside the girl next to her and get their faces as close to the recruits as they could without touching her. She was taking too long. The drill instructors were quiet because they didn't want to alarm the relatives on the other end. The girl got the hint and ended her call.

After five rings, the answering machine at Cassie's parents' house picked up. "Mom, I made it to Paris Island safely. Bye." Click.

As Cassie turned from the phone, a drill instructor ordered her to, "Follow the yellow line to the next station. Move!"

Cassie followed the yellow line to the next room. The décor of the second room was similar to the first. Female Marine privates operated ten measuring stations. At least one girl waited in line at each station. Cassie stepped up to the shortest line. A Marine Corps private handed Cassie a clipboard with a blank measuring form on it. In two minutes, all of Cassie's physical measurements were taken and recorded: height, inseam, bust, waist, hips, nose-to-fingertip, fingertip-to-fingertip, shoe size, hat size.

"Follow the yellow line!"

The third room was larger, the size of a high school lunchroom, and had the same grey walls and green tile floors. Four counters, which reminded Cassie of airport security check in stations, filled the first half of the room. Behind the counters was a dizzying array of boxes, racks of uniforms, and stacks of eight-point digital utility hats. A lance corporal handed Cassie a bin for her first Marine clothing issue: boots, size seven; two digital eight-point field caps, size six and a quarter; four pairs of small wool socks; four sets underwear; two tan utility belts, twenty-six inches; and so on. Cassie received everything that she would need to change out of her civvies and into the standard-issue, Marine utility uniform called digitals.

Cassie collected her new issue and walked to the second half of the expansive room. She thought that the space was comical and from an old prison movie. The prominent feature in the room was the walkway, raised four feet off the floor. Two female Marine sergeants looked like prison guards as they walked back and forth on the walkway, watching the trainees in the changing booths. A dozen narrow changing booths with waist-high walls lined the raised walkway on either side. In each booth, a girl was changing into her first Marine uniform.

The sergeants watched for contraband, including electronic devices, weapons, drugs, forbidden foods, and much more. This changing space marked a boundary. One of the sergeants on the walkway repeated a paragraph of instruction.

"From here on, we will not tolerate contraband items. Possession of a contraband item is grounds for being pulled from the program, discharged from the Marines, and, possibly, facing criminal charges."

The two sergeants also coached the recruits on wearing the field digital uniform properly. Marine recruiters had shown most of the recruits how to wear the digital uniform during the selection process. But every now and again, the two sergeants had to coach one of the screw-ups.

"Re-lace those boots properly, you're not in a fashion show. Button that shirt all the way to the top, we don't want to see your cleavage. Pull those pants up around your waist, you're not in east L.A."

Cassie shed her civilian clothes and put on her digitals. As she worked, she was aware of big sister watching. The sounds of women changing clothes created a gentle din in the room. Cassie tried to be as quiet and as fast as possible. Still, she couldn't help but overhear the Marine to Cassie's right whispering to the recruit to her right.

"You better wipe that deer-in-the-headlights look off your face. The drill instructors are looking for signs of weakness. They'll target you. Your face screams, 'I'm scared. I'm a quitter.' If you're weak, the drill instructors will want to wash you out and not waste time and resources on you. Worse yet, they don't want to pass a weakling through who might buckle, quit, or endanger someone else later. Now, buck up. You made it this far because a lot of people knew you have what it takes to be a Marine. Pull up those tan utility boxers and start acting like a Marine recruit. And, for God's sake, put your growl on."

A female private stepped up behind Cassie, "Are you finished? Stand up and turn around."

The private had a small pair of scissors in her hand. She examined Cassie's uniform with a practiced precision and cut off even the tiniest threads (skin tags, to use the vernacular) that stuck out from Cassie's new uniform.

"Your uniform will be kept serviceable and neat at all times. We call these hanging threads Irish Pennants. You will examine your uniform daily and remove all Irish Pennants. Irish Pennants are an indication of a sloppy Marine and a lazy mind." The private inspected the rest of Cassie's uniform. "Blouse cuffs will be buttoned or rolled at all times. Unbuttoned or hanging cuffs won't be tolerated."

Cassie buttoned her cuffs and decided not to try to explain that she just hadn't gotten that far yet. No excuses.

"No unlisted personal items or listed contraband items beyond this point, no exceptions. You must discard all such items or put them into this envelope to be stored until you leave for your next duty station. Is that clear?"

"I have no personal items to check."

Cassie didn't have to add a specific title on the end of her statement. The young woman holding the envelope had earned no such title. She wasn't a sergeant, an officer, or a drill instructor. Cassie declined the envelope. She scooped up her civilian clothes and deposited them in the trash bin. Cassie had nothing else with her that she had owned for more than five minutes. She had sent her driver's license, a small iPod, and six dollars home before getting on the bus earlier that afternoon. As of this moment, like the other recruits, Cassie had been stripped of her past, personal identity.

"Follow the yellow line."

Cassie followed the yellow line into another large supply room.

At the first table, a private first class asked, "Name?"

"Cassandra Sing."

The private handed Recruit Sing two Marine-issued, digital duffle bags with the name "Sing, C." stenciled on the reinforced, canvas handles.

The PFC looked at Recruit Sing and said in a faint voice, "Do yourself a favor. Next time, answer, 'Recruit Sing, Cassandra.' Follow the yellow line."

Recruit Sing stepped up to the first table she came to on the yellow line. A poster on the wall showed the marine technique for folding the sides of a duffle bag down like the sleeves of an upside-down shirtsleeve. After the fold, the duffle bag formed a square, six-inch-deep canvas bowl, and for the next ten minutes, Recruit Sing received Marine Corps issued equipment and uniforms. As Recruit Sing received each item, the issuing clerk showed Recruit Sing how to fold and arrange the items in her duffle bags. As the bags filled, Recruit Sing unrolled the sides upward to keep the inside of the bag a uniform six inches deep.

After receiving her initial issue, Recruit Sing followed the yellow line out the back door of the receiving center. She carried everything she owned in two duffle bags that held a combined weight of eighty pounds.

A drill instructor with a clipboard stood by the door. She asked, "Name?"

"Recruit Sing, Cassandra, Drill Instructor," Cassie answered. She was no longer just *Cassie.*

The drill instructor consulted her clipboard, "Do you have any contraband items or unapproved personal items?"

"No, Drill Instructor."

The drill instructor gestured to one of the groups of recruits and said quietly, "You're in Bravo Company, get in line. Relax until ordered to fall in. You may converse with the others, quietly!"

Recruit Sing joined the ranks of the Bravo Company, set her duffle bags on the asphalt, and joined the muted conversations nearest her.

"Hi, I'm Jill."

"I'm Rosa."

Recruit Sing smiled a little and said, "I'm Recruit Sing."

The others looked at Cassie until one said, "I'm *Recruit* Reynolds."

Another followed suit, "I'm *Recruit* Hernandez."

The recruits seemed to think the new distinction was amusing. The episode broke the tension. Recruit Sing looked around the gathering a second time. Everything had changed. In one night, the Marine Corps had swept away most of the characteristics that made the recruits different from each other. None of the recruits could tell whose father was a lawyer and whose father was a laborer. There was no indication of who came from money and who came from poverty. No recruit wore a more expensive uniform than any other recruit. The induction process had eliminated most of the individual differences that the Marine Corps didn't value.

There were still physical differences which the Marine Corps couldn't eliminate, so the Corps accepted them. As Recruit Sing perused the group, she realized that when everyone was different, the differences don't matter.

The recruits were on an even playing field, now. They all had the same chance to succeed or fail, and they would succeed or fail by their own efforts. They couldn't blame anyone else. In a few hours, the two companies of recruits would begin the transformation into a Marine Unit. Ninety-six young women had walked into the reception center last night. Ninety-six Marine Corps recruits walked out. Recruit Sing liked what she saw. She was beginning to feel at home. She was beginning to feel a part of that elusive something.

"Fall in."

The drill instructor didn't have to say it twice.

After the recruits moved into formation and settled down, the drill instructor said, "All recruits bring your duffle bags to this line and stack them neatly." Two flatbed, field utility trucks sat next to the line. "I want two volunteers from each company, front and center."

Friends and relatives had warned the recruits not to volunteer. For a few seconds, no one moved. Eventually, two recruits stepped forward from each company. Cassie assumed that the volunteers would be loading the duffle bags onto the trucks.

The drill instructor pointed to the ground next to her. "Volunteers stand here."

Once the volunteers had formed a line next to the drill instructor, she addressed the rest of the recruits. "When I give the order, all of you will fall out and load the duffle bags on the trucks and then return to your ranks. You will have thirty seconds. Do you understand?"

The recruits screamed, "Yes, Drill Instructor!"

"Load the trucks!"

The recruits' attempts to load the trucks were a jumbled chaos that took a minute and fifteen seconds.

When the ranks were quiet, the drill instructor announced, "One minute and fifteen seconds. Unload the trucks and restack the duffle bags. Move! Move!"

The four volunteers watched from the sidelines as the recruits repeated the process two more times before they loaded the trucks in under thirty seconds. They were learning to work together.

When the ranks reformed, the drill instructor turned to the four volunteers and ordered, "Two of you will ride on the back of each truck and guard the duffle bags. Mount up."

As the four volunteers made themselves comfortable on the backs of the trucks, the drill instructor turned back to the formations and announced, "If you don't learn how to act as a coordinated team, you will fail at Paris Island. To make sure that you understand this concept, we are going on a five-mile training run before we go to your barracks. Atten...shun! Right... face! Forward... march. Double time... march!"

Welcome to the Marines.

*****

At first, all Cassie could see from her hiding place in the desert was the back gate and taillights of the deuce and a half as it pulled into the parking area. As soon as the truck was halfway into the yard, Cassie noticed something startling in the terrain. The truck made a sweeping right turn around a quarter-acre, white gravel parking area. It wasn't just a rough, gravel parking lot. It was a brand new, professionally spread, graded, rolled, and compacted parking area that looked more like aggregated concrete. The deuce didn't leave a mark in the surface as it turned.

A third of the way around the left edge of the parking area was a small, original, one-room hunting cabin. It was unpainted, with no porch, and shaded windows. Interior light showed through holes and gaps in the corrugated tin roof. In some places, a crack of light or two showed around the edges of some of the windows. Cassie heard a loud sporting event playing on a TV or radio inside the cabin. A 200-gallon water tank stood on stilts next to the cabin. A car and two pickup trucks were parked in front.

On the far right-hand edge of the parking area was a tall, doublewide, pole barn. The barn also looked like an original structure. It had a unique feature that caught Cassie's attention: a shiny, new, twenty-foot-tall, aluminum rollup door mounted on one end. The new door made the barn look decrepit by comparison. *Either the weight of the door will collapse the barn, or the door must be holding the barn up*, Cassie thought. The barn was lit up like a surgical suite: light poured out around several flaws in the siding, roof, and windows.

When she focused on the barn, Cassie heard the roar of a gasoline generator from behind the cabin. From the amount of lighting, Cassie knew that the generator must be larger than a skid-mounted, consumer gas generator. These men were using a lot of electricity.

On the far side of the parking area was what must have been the original improved yard for the property. The small yard was between the cabin and barn and defined the character of the property and the previous owner. Piles of debris, junk, and forgotten treasures dotted the area. She could see a jumbled pile of railroad ties with grass growing between the timbers. There were several piles of old engine blocks and transmissions, and there was the obligatory pickup truck frame on blocks without wheels.

People hadn't lived on this property before these men took over. They had visited from time to time. This was a hunter's hooch. Hunters would come to the cabin the evening before a day of hunting. They'd play cards, clean guns, tell stories, and drink too much alcohol. The whole arrangement allowed the hunters to get a pre-dawn start on the game birds in the area. A night in the cabin was far better than a thirty-minute drive from town in the morning. These weekend warriors convinced themselves it was necessary to use every advantage possible to bag their limit of wild turkeys and pheasants.

The driver of the deuce and a half honked his horn several times as the truck made the sweeping turn to the right. The cabin door flew open, and a cascade of light and sound flooded the parking lot. Four men came out of the cabin. All four carried silenced, automatic pistols. The truck continued until it was in front of the barn's rollup door. The driver stopped and waited for the men from the cabin to open the rollup door so he could back inside. The well-lit truck was facing Cassie now. She could see three men in the truck. They wore regulation Army fatigue shirts. The man (women?) in the middle was shorter than the other two. The driver had a short-cropped flat top haircut.

*****

The Special Weapons Storage Facility sat in a concealed depression between three small hills in far western and largely deserted reaches of Fort Sill. It was a squat, featureless, grey bunker of a building, at least on the surface. Below ground, there were several stories of concrete hallways, workshops, and a maze of shielded weapons storage bays. Any unusual event (especially a full base lockdown) at Fort Sill triggered a mandatory weapons inventory. Two Special Weapons Ordinance NCOs double-checked the results of the latest inventory.

"That can't be correct. We can't have lost two weapons in the last two weeks."

"We didn't lose anything. Two W-63's were designated as retired this afternoon. They were supposed to be transferred from the maintenance facility this afternoon. They were signed out of maintenance at 14:12 this afternoon. They never arrived."

"Damn, somebodies' ass is going to fry for this one. I'm glad it wasn't our screw-up."

One of the NCO's stepped over to a facility only, landline and dialed the ops center's number. Radios and/or phones didn't work in the facility, much less this far underground.

*****

Cassie noticed that no guard had come out of the desert to join the group. She didn't know what to make of the mistake. *Are they so arrogant that they don't see the need to post a guard at the head of the driveway or at the edge of the parking area?*

Either these weren't trained military, or the guard was trained well enough that he hadn't shown himself.

As the deuce and a half backed into the barn, Cassie glimpsed the nose of a light blue, commercial semi-truck already in the barn. The door rolled down and sealed itself against the barn's floor. Cassie seemed to be alone, but she was always one to be cautious. She remained as still as possible for several minutes, watching the virgin desert around the edge of the parking area for a guard. Eventually, the sounds of the night desert played again. A field mouse searching the ground between piles of junk caught Cassis eye. She saw no glowing cigarette embers or heard any muffled cough. She received her first real break. No guards outside meant that she had only seven armed terrorists to confront, not eight.

The undisturbed ground beyond the gravel parking lot to Cassie's right was flat and had a sparse growth of knee-high grass covering it. She would have to crawl on her belly to conceal herself.

To Cassie's left, the ground between her and the cabin had small rises and scattered clumps of brush. This suited Cassie more. She needed to check out the cabin for lingering members of the gang. She didn't like surprises. She also wanted to check the vehicles and the cabin for a phone or a gun. She desperately wanted to call her chain of command for reinforcements and didn't want to confront these men armed with only her good looks and charm.

She took a shallow breath and unclipped the shoulder straps of her canvas fire bibs. The bibs had several strips of reflective safety tape designed to make the firefighters more visible when on a fire scene. She had her digital pants and a tan t-shirt under her bibs.

Cassie said a short prayer of thanks to her guardian angel. She had worn her utility boots to the grass fire. Once she dropped the bibs, she wore digital, Marine-issue camouflage.

Cassie moved to her left, keeping as low to the grass as she could. She tried not to move her upper body any more than necessary. When she reached the next clump of brush, she froze and listened to the night. All she heard was the far-off call of a lone, Great Horned owl. Cassie wasn't hunting alone tonight.

She moved a second time without incident, but as she started her crawl a third time, she saw a slight shift in the shadows by the back of the cabin. She froze, holding her breath. Cassie dithered her eyes as the Marines had taught her to improve her night vision. She heard the muffled conversations of the men in the barn and the rumble of the generator close by. She felt the cool night air on her neck. The movement came again. Another tiny field mouse scurried across the sand. Cassie resumed breathing, crept behind another bush, and surveyed the area. She needed to relax or she wasn't going to make it to the cabin.

Cassie emerged from the dark brush at the back of the cabin like a slow-moving specter. She approached the largest opening in the window coverings and swayed her head back and forth in long, sweeping arcs so she could see as much of the interior as possible with each step. She didn't want to find herself eye-to-eye with one of the men.

By the time she got close to the glass, she could see most of the interior of the cabin. It was deserted. All seven of her adversaries were in the barn. The inside of the cabin was starker than she had imagined. The walls and vaulted ceiling had no insulation or sheetrock, the exact interior was one big room with two doors at the far end, perhaps a bathroom and small storage closet. Cassie hadn't seen an outhouse. A minimum of permanent electrical wiring was stapled to the wall studs.

The men had pulled an orange electrical cord through a window from the generator. The cord ended at a large, industrial-sized power strip on the floor. A microwave, a refrigerator, and a flat screen television were plugged into it. The basketball game that Cassie heard earlier was still playing. Several fold-up aluminum chairs were huddled around the TV, and some blowup airbeds stood on end in the corner. These guys had either already been here or were planning on staying a while.

She looked around the room again. There was no landline telephone. Considering the remoteness of the cabin, Cassie knew that it was a small possibility anyway. She had hoped for a satellite phone, but neither that nor a cell phone was visible. She didn't see any guns. What she wouldn't give for a gun of her own now. She didn't see any car keys either.

Cassie worked her way around the cabin to the parking area. She was ten feet from the car, but she knew that her best bet for finding a gun was in one of the pickup trucks, under the driver's seat or in the glove compartment. She kept the vehicles between her and the barn as she stepped up to the farthest truck. The windows were up, and the doors were locked, so she couldn't take a chance on the alarm. She didn't touch the truck but scanned the inside for later reference. The interior of the truck was immaculate. There was nothing to see.

She crept to the second truck. The windows were down, and the doors were unlocked. She still couldn't open the doors because she didn't want the interior light to come on, so she stepped up onto the driver's side running board, leaned into the cab as far as she could, and felt along the space between the door and the seat.; nothing. She reached under the driver's seat. Again, nothing. She dropped back to the gravel and moved to the front of the truck. If she checked the passenger side of the truck, she'd be visible to anyone who might come out of the barn. This search had to be fast. She quick-stepped to the passenger's door, stepped up onto the passenger side running board, and leaned into the truck as far as she could. She popped the glove compartment and found nothing but a half a dozen discarded traffic tickets. She reached under the seat and came up with a handful of trash. There was no phone in the center console or the ashtray. She dropped back to the gravel and faded back into the shadows.

Cassie didn't hold out much hope of finding anything in the car, but she looked anyway. Men who drove pickup trucks usually carried guns. Men who drove four-door family cars weren't prone to keeping guns. Again, the windows were up, and the doors were locked. A quick glance told Cassie that she would find nothing useful in the car. It too, was cleaner than expected.

She retraced her steps around the cabin and headed to the open debris field between the cabin and the barn. She needed to know what was going on in the barn. She hunkered down and walked along a narrow strip of clear ground along the edge of the property.

She didn't have to worry about being quiet. Between the blaring music in the barn, the shouts of the men, and the roaring of the generator, Cassie could have driven a Hummer up to the barn and not be heard from inside. She took note of one positive feature of the barn: no doors opened to the desert side of the barn. There was no reason for any of the men to come around to where she was crouched. She felt as comfortable as could be expected as she approached the largest opening in the side.

Cassie peered through the crack in the loose siding. All Cassie could see was the side of a silver, commercial tanker truck emblazoned with Comanche County Dairy Corporation. Next to the name was a smiling cartoon caricature of a contented cow. The tanker truck hid Cassie's view of the rest of the interior. She moved further along the side of the barn and found an opening low down on the siding that afforded her a view of the back of the two trucks. She found herself looking out from underneath a workbench with a clear view of the open area inside the barn.

The wooden structure of the barn looked like it was one hundred years old. Years of accumulated grease, grime, and sweat stained the wood. Everything was a dull, oily black except for the four new poles of the tall a-frame straddling the open area behind the trucks. The a-frame's timbers were pristine and supported a new engine crane with a rail and traversing rollers at the top. The floor of the barn was loose dirt but didn't give up any dust as the men moved around. The floor had been soaked black by years of cast-off crud.

Cassie understood why the men hadn't posted a guard. The seven of them were all hard at work. They couldn't spare anyone for outside guard duty. Every man seemed to know his job and every man was busy.

Chapter Twelve

The Major was directing three men who were working on the deuce and a half. The men had released the tie-downs on the truck's canvas cover and rolled it forward, exposing the back half of the truck bed. They had also removed the rearmost two support ribs. The bed was open for the crane to access the truck's cargo. Cassie had always thought the big Army trucks looked like beetles with the canvas covers in place. With the cover removed and the ribs showing, Cassie thought that the truck looked like something dead and decaying in the desert.

The other three men were working at the back of the milk truck. The man with the flat top haircut directed their work. He was the one who had been driving the deuce and a half and had killed the two Army gate guards. Cassie concentrated on him for a minute. She studied every feature of his face and mannerisms. She wanted to be sure that she could pick him out of lineup later.

While Flat Top and his two assistants were working on an apparatus on the ground, Cassie inspected the milk tanker truck. A skilled metalworker had modified the shiny dome that formed the back of the tank. He had cut a precise two-foot hole in the center of the dome and reinstalled a cutaway dome over the hole using two hinges. The designer mounted one hinge on either side of the small dome. The men had removed the lynchpin from the left hinge, allowing it swing open on the right hinge. They could have removed the right linchpin and swung the door open to left if they had wanted. Closed and with both lynchpins inserted, the small dome fit perfectly into the hole in the large dome. Cassie guessed that the door wasn't watertight (or milk tight), but a casual observer driving next to the milk truck on the highway might not notice the hinges or the extra seam on the back of the main tank.

It was a clever design, but it didn't make much sense. Any liquid put into the tank would slosh out every time the driver changed the direction or speed of the truck. A gushing, open leak in the middle of the back dome of a tanker truck on the highway would catch the attention of every driver on the road. There had to be more.

Cassie was lying on the ground near the crack in the siding at the bottom of the wall. She was looking up and more from the side of the truck than from behind, so she didn't have unobstructed of the modified hatch. After studying the opening, she realized that, when she looked into the hole, she wasn't looking into the dark interior of the large tank. She was looking at the inside surface of a secondary tank that had been inserted into the hole and welded into place. The smaller tank was the same diameter as the hole in the dome. Cassie couldn't tell how deep the secondary tank might be, but she guessed the space was deep enough to hold two contraband nuclear weapons. The inside tank was a dry *smuggler's hold* inside of the normal truck tank. If no one noticed the hinges or the radiation, the terrorists would be home free.

The Major's crew worked for a few minutes to lower the first shipping skeleton to the ground between the trucks. Once the nuke was in place and disconnected, The Major and his crew took the crane back to the deuce and a half and connected the second nuke. These men knew what they were doing and had practiced their roles.

Flat Top's crew removed the top structures and straps from the shipping skeleton. Cassie watched them for a few seconds, then turned her attention to the homemade stand on the ground behind the milk truck. The stand looked like a ten-foot section of an oversized bowling ball return. Several smooth tubes ran close together along the length to make a two-foot-wide and ten-foot-long trough. The end of the tubes formed the bottom half of a circle. The stand had a lifting eye at each of the corners.

Half of an eight-foot-long, rough-cut Styrofoam cylinder lay in the bowling ball trough. The builder had cut the original cylinder in half down the long axis. The flat side of the cylinder that faced up was no longer a smooth, flat surface. The cylinder's maker had gouged a cavity in the surface with a chisel or a large spoon. A small lifting eye stuck out of the end of the Styrofoam just above the metal of the cradle.

Flat Top's crew removed enough of the skeleton structure to expose the first nuke without loosening the bottom support structures. The Major and his crew set the second nuke next to the first and disconnected the lifting clamps. Flat Top's crew used simple canvas straps to lift the first nuke away from the skeleton without placing too much stress on the remaining support structure. When they removed the last of the support bolts, the nuke swung free of the skeleton. It was simple to lift the nuke free and place it in the waiting Styrofoam cradle.

The Major's men pulled the remains of the first skeleton further into the barn and out of the way of the workers, and then they muscled the second nuke into place between the trucks. Once The Major was satisfied with the placement, he and his crew went back to work on the deuce and a half.

Flat Top picked up the second half of the Styrofoam cylinder and placed it flat side down over the nuke. The completed Styrofoam clamshell formed a protective cy-lindrical case. One of the men strung half a dozen plastic tie-wraps around the cylinder to keep it from coming apart, then pulled the crane over the bowling trough and connected the straps to the lifting eyes. They raised the round bowling trough and aligned it with the smuggler's hold in the milk tank. One of the men pushed the Styrofoam-encased nuke into the hold as far as he could reach. Then, Flat Top used a length of four-by-four to push the cylinder to the deepest end of the hold.

Cassie thought that he looked like a civil war soldier ramming a powder charge into a field cannon.

Flat Top and his crew started on the second nuke. Cassie thought that The Major and his crew would just put the deuce and a half back together and leave it at that, but when she looked back at the truck, she knew that she was wrong. The Major and his men loaded three empty, fifty-five-gallon steel barrels onto the bed of the truck and secured them to the truck's cargo tie-down eyes. They filled the drums with dry, high-Nitrogen fertilizer. Several cans of diesel fuel were on the ground by the rear wheels of the truck.

Oh my God. They're making a fertilizer bomb--a big fertilizer bomb!

Occasionally, the men dropped a double handful of nails and ball bearings into the mix. They designed a bomb that would kill everyone within twenty to thirty yards. Cassie watched the men tape a stick of dynamite on the inside of each lid and then place the lids on the barrels. One man then wired the three lids to a box with a length of cable. Cassie couldn't see enough of the box to determine if it was a push button detonator or a timer.

Whatever the box was, Cassie didn't have time for it. It was time to go. She knew that she couldn't confront seven armed men alone. If the men captured or killed her, there would be no one to call in the military, and they might get away. She retraced her steps around the barn, passed the piles of debris, crept behind the cabin and through the light stands of brush to her starting place. She started walking down the edge of the driveway. She estimated that she had been at the cabin for two hours. It *must be close to midnight.* She had to get back to the highway and flag down some help. Once she was out of sight of the barn, she ran.

Chapter Thirteen

By 9:30 p.m., the military police officer in charge (MP-OIC) at the Military Operations Office, Fort Sill, was busy acting as a central clearinghouse for all information coming in from the field. During an attack, or a suspected attack, the MP-OIC decided what information was important and what information to ignore. He also decided what pieces of information might be pieced to threads of other information. His job was as intense as the process of conducting a six-month long murder investigation in two hours.

From the sea of olive drab uniforms and bobbing heads, a voice rose above the din and reported, "Weapons inventory underway at the weapons maintenance and weapons storage facility."

The MP-OIC nodded to the specialist who gave the report.

"Drone flyover of north firing ranges show no activity," reported another voice.

The MP-OIC nodded again.

"Main gate and east highway gate report no unusual activity."

"All housing areas locked down."

"All central command officers accounted for."

"No activity on west perimeter."

"The Nuclear Ordinance Maintenance Facility reports no activity."

"Sir," a senior NCO said next to the MP-OIC's shoulder.

The MP-OIC turned to the NCO and focused his full attention on the sergeant.

"Nuclear Training Command reported that a Lance Corporal Cassandra Sing, USMC went missing without explanation at approximately twenty thirty hours from the training command while fighting a small grass fire outside the north perimeter. Her last known location is one mile from the Fort Sill north gate. They don't know if the two incidents are related. They will keep us advised."

The MP-OIC answered, "Thank you, Sergeant."

The MP-OIC took a moment to recall the name Cassandra Sing. Lance Corporal Sing was a family member of a high-ranking presidential DHS advisor, Brian Sing. As OIC Fourth Army Command, he had a standing order to know the status of all relatives of high-risk targets within the Fourth Army Theater of Operation. An unknown person or group might have kidnapped Lance Corporal Sing. That person or group might try to use the kidnapping as leverage to influence Mr. Sing.

The MP-OIC raised his hand into the air and announced, "Everybody, up here."

Instantly, the noise in the room ceased and every head turned toward the MP-OIC. One could have heard a pin drop.

In a normal voice, the MP-OIC said, "One Lance Corporal Cassandra Sing, USMC is missing without explanation from the Ordinance Training Command. Lance Corporal Sing is on our Priority Security Watch list. Notify all search teams and all operations commands to be on the lookout for Lance Corporal Sing. Find her!"

The MP-OIC put his hand down. The cacophonous flow of operating information resumed. The MP-OIC picked up his phone, stepped to the back of the command center and called General Marks' Executive Officer. He knew that General Marks would call Mr. Sing personally.

"Base hospital locked down and searched. Base Hospital is operational. Guards have been posted."

A communications NCO stepped up to the MP-OIC and said with a secretive manner, "Sir, Weapons Maintenance reports that two W-63, warheads were cleared from

the Weapons Maintenance Depot this afternoon for transfer to the long-term storage
facility. They never arrived at the storage facility."

*****

General Marks called Brian Sing's
aide's Government Issue cell. Brian Sing was
the kind of presidential advisor that warranted a personal phone call when there was less
than good news. Brian was unusual in that he
didn't buy his appointment by contributing
more to the president's campaign coffers
than any other politician. Brian wasn't a political appointee that held more fundraisers
than his competition. The president trusted
and supported Brian Sing because Brian was
independent. He owed no affiliation to any
political party or special-interest group. No
political PAC or lobby owned him. Neither
big business nor the war industry pulled his
strings. He was a true free voice. When Brian
advised the president, the president knew that
Brian's advice was in the best interest of the
country.

Brian was an eight-year veteran of the
U.S. Army Nuclear Power Program, head-
quartered at Fort Belvoir, Virginia, and had
an advanced degree in nuclear engineering.
Brian also had a knack for popping up in the

middle of an investigation whenever the crime involved nuclear-based terrorism. He had been an operations supervisor at the Desert Canyons Nuclear Power Station in California and had made the pivotal decisions that kept radioactive contamination from spreading outside the power plant proper. He had saved SoCal from radioactive contamination on a statewide scale. Brian was a senior scientist at the Madam Curie National Laboratory outside Seattle, Washington when spies hacked the secure servers that held the libraries of our nation's nuclear weapons programs. He led the team of cyber investigators that traced the theft to the Chinese Ministry of State Security.

Brian was the technical advisor credited with neutralizing the threat to contaminate the White House with radioactive dirty bomb. Brian's insights led to the capture of the entire terror cell. His most unusual assignment was as the technical asset assigned to a CIA team investigating the source of naturally occurring, radioactive gold found in the Zamfara River in Northern Nigeria. Gold doesn't occur in nature in the radioactive state.

During each situation, Brian provided sound intelligence, situation analysis, and

advice to the president. The president considered Brian one of his top and most trusted
advisors on all matters of homeland security,
particularly when nuclear materials are involved.

Tonight, Brian's knack exerted itself
once again. He was attending a conference
for the department heads of the twenty-four
major branches of the Department of Homeland Security at the Dallas Fort Worth Convention Center.

Chapter Fourteen

The Sam Houston Conference Room wasn't the largest room at the Dallas Fort Worth Convention Center. The maximum capacity was thirty. Even for thirty, space was tight. The black conference table gave the impression of close confidence, and the central lighting made the group seem more intimate. One door opened out into the atrium. There was no service door at the back of the conference room because the convention center didn't provide catering services in the room. Coffee, tea, and water were available on a side table. This was the most secure room at the convention center.

Two Department of Homeland Security officers stood guard outside the meeting room door, waiting for the current meeting to end. It was 10:40 p.m. and it had been a long day. The access atrium was wide and lavish, decorated with gold filigree and red carpet. The three chandeliers, high overhead, were impressive. The atrium was so big that the guards almost blended into the décor. Two more guards stood just out of sight at either end of the atrium. The meeting attendees warranted the extra level of security. Brian called for everyone's attention so he could close the proceedings.

"Ladies and Gentlemen... ladies and gentlemen, I will include your comments and suggestions in my report to the president. I want to wrap this meeting by quantifying, one more time, the new presidential operating directives for Homeland Security. In the past, our objective was to watch and monitor all persons of interest to homeland security to obtain as much intelligence as possible. On a few occasions, we were so busy monitoring the subjects that some of them slipped our surveillance and committed acts of terrorism inside the United States. We have refined our intelligence expertise to the point that the intelligence we garnished by over-monitoring persons of interest led only to people or organizations that we already had on our radar. Over-monitoring didn't produce a proportional measure of new intelligence. No more. As of today, we are adopting a new strategy: the three directives.

"Directive one mandates that we prevent, at all costs, the completion of an act of terrorism against the people or the property of the United States; no more shopping mall shootings, no more bombings, no more plane crashes. The first directive also dictates that all suspected acts of terrorism be neutralized at the earliest possible time. No act of terrorism will be allowed to progress past the moment that it is first detected.

"Directive Two states that all persons suspected of planning or carrying out an act of terrorism will be apprehended and prosecuted without exception. The American intelligence community will no longer try to turn or use suspected terrorists to capture other suspected terrorists. The process hasn't been productive in reducing terrorist threats. Directive Two will be attempted if, and only if, it doesn't interfere with the absolute and total compliance with Directive One."

Once again, Brian couldn't but help notice the similarities between the president's three directives of homeland security and Isaac Asimov's three laws of robotics. Brian wondered if the president was a sci-fi fan.

"Directive Three will be applied if and only if the first two directives can be completed with 100 percent success. The third directive requires the continued preservation of the peaceful, tranquil, and secure state of mind enjoyed by all Americans. The first priority of the Third Directive is to eliminate the terrorist threat and arrest all conspirators in such a way that the American public and American news media never know about the operation. The president doesn't want the average American losing sleep because there are too many overly sensationalized terrorist incidents flooding the news. The president wants the average American man and woman to feel safe and secure in their daily lives.

"If the public or the news media becomes aware of the takedown of a terrorist plot, then we want that take down to be as high profile as possible: SWAT troops, flash bangs, machine guns, helicopters, and armored vehicles. We want the public to see that we are aggressively and successfully crushing any perceived terrorist threat to the people. Again, we want them to believe that there's nothing to fear. There's no need to lose sleep. Homeland Security is efficiently and effectively keeping our homeland secure."

Brian was about to close the meeting and release the participants when one of his aides stepped to his side and got his attention.

"One moment, please."

Brian showed no negative facial reaction as the aide handed him a folded note. It read:

June 15, 2050 hours.

Mr. Sing,

At 2030 hours, Lance Corporal Cassandra Sing went missing without explanation from a firefighting detail while fighting a grass fire outside the north perimeter of Fort Sill, Oklahoma. At approximately the same time, unknown assailants murdered two MP gate guards at the Fort Sill north gate. The assailants used a commandeered Army truck in the incident. Two W-63 warheads are also missing. Unknown if the incidents are related. Investigation continues. Will keep you posted. Call if you have questions. 1-580-555-1211.

Major General Omar Marks, Fourth Army Commanding.

Brian turned to his aide and said in an even voice, "Have a helicopter meet me on the roof in fifteen minutes."

The aide started to speak, but Brian cut him off, "Make it a fast helicopter. I may be keeping it for a couple of days."

Brian turned on his heel and left the conference room.

The aide stepped to the microphone and said, "Mr. Sing has been called away. This meeting is adjourned."

Ten minutes later, Brian Sing emerged onto the conference center rooftop heliport with a small overnight bag in his hand. A Sikorsky S-300 helicopter was waiting with the rotors idling. The star and eagle of The United States Marshalls Service was acid-etched into the doors of the passenger bubble. Brian would be at Fort Sill by zero one thirty hours.

Chapter Fifteen

Inside the barn, the terrorists were completing the last few tasks on the deuce and a half. The men had restored the canvas cover over the truck's bed. It looked like a big, olive-green beetle again. The men had strung the bombs' control cable and box into the cab. It lay on the passenger's seat like a discarded rope.

The Major walked up to one of the other men and said, "Stevens, it's time to go."

Stevens stood up and dropped the rag that he was wiping his hands on and said, "Yes, Sir."

"Tell me your assignment again."

Stevens recited his instructions for the thousandth time. "Drive to downtown Amarillo, Texas. I will park the truck in the underground garage of J. Marvin Jones Federal Building, if possible. I will push the button on the control box to arm the bomb. I will have three minutes to get as far away as possible. If I can't get far enough away in the three minutes, I can push the button a second time to stop the timer. If I push the button a third time, the timer will start over. The explosion will signal the start of the second revolution. Brother organizations around the country will recognize the call and take up the fight. We will restore the Constitution.

"There is little chance that I will make it all the way to Amarillo. The police and the military will be looking for this truck and will try to stop me. If the authorities do stop me, I'll try to make it to a non-threatening public area. I will wait until as many police and news crews are on site as possible. I will arm the timer for the bomb and get as far from the truck as I can. The result will be the same. The explosion will signal the start of the revolution."

"Good," said The Major. "Good." The Major placed a hand on Stevens' shoulder. "You're doing a great thing today, Stevens. You'll be heralded as a hero, Son. Don't stop for anything. Don't trust anybody. Up you go."

Stevens climbed into the driver's seat, put his gun on the seat, and pulled the control box closer to him. He found comfort in the presence of the heavy control box and its internal timer. He didn't feel so alone in the truck. He started the truck and waited for the roll up door to clear the top of his canopy. Yes, Stevens was elated and savored the rush of pure joy that he felt. This would be the opening act of violence in a greater war. He was grateful beyond measure that The Major had chosen him to be the first combatant on the field.

Down deep, Stevens was also afraid. He was afraid that he wouldn't be able to complete his mission honorably. He was afraid of what the authorities would do to him before the revolution gained momentum and before The Major set him free. He felt the bile in him rise. He wanted to be away from the rest of the crew before his over-strung nerves got the better of him.

The Major watched the deuce and half roll away with a contemptuous smile on his face. *Too bad,* thought the Major. *Stevens was a nice kid; gullible, but nice.* The Major smiled an evil sneer because he knew the truth about the truck, the fake timer, and the suicide driver.

There was no timer. The circuit boards and heavy transformer in the box were a ruse. The Major had rigged the button as a dead-man's switch. When Stevens pushed the spring-loaded button, the trigger would arm itself. When Stevens released the button the first time, the bomb would deto-nate instantly. Even if the operator was dead, the spring-release would push the button out and trigger the bomb. Stevens and the truck bomb were an elaborate diversion to buy the time necessary for The Major and Flat Top to get away.

The Major knew that it was monstrous of him to send this simpleton to certain death for no more than a diversion. He regretted having to deceive the boy into thinking that he was committing an act of heroism, but the regret didn't last long. As soon as The Major let his mind drift to the soft retirement that the two nukes would provide, his harder, greedier side pushed its way to the surface.

Stevens was nothing to The Major. Stevens didn't exhibit more than a second-grade education. He had no natural intelligence and was only able to parrot the intelligent statements of others. The Major also suspected that Stevens had an I.Q. of no higher than eighty-five or ninety. There was just not a lot to work with there. In The Major's opinion, Stevens would never amount to more than a lifetime of chronic welfare. One thought did assuage The Major's brief feelings of pity: he felt he was doing society a favor by eliminating Stevens now.

The Major did face one dilemma about using Stevens: the opinions of the other revolutionaries. They wouldn't react kindly to the idea that he was going to be sacrificed in a few hours. He was going to die the inglorious death of a worthless ort of collateral damage. The only other person who knew that the box was a trigger and not a timer, was Flat Top. The Major told the others that he selected Stevens for this mission because he believed in him. The others believed that The Major wanted to give Stevens a part in the revolution that would leave him with a sense of patriotism and accomplishment.

The Major pointed out that, even though Stevens wasn't the smartest member of the crew, he could still recognize the truth and logic of The Major's words. Stevens couldn't formulate the words himself, but he could recognize the validity of The Major's. The Major often said, "It's for the Stevens' of America that we're starting this revolution. We'll tell them the truth about their government. Just like Stevens, they'll know that our words are true. The government just rolls over people like Stevens, uses them, and discards them. It's up to us to provide a better life for the Stevens around us. We value the meek of the world."

Words were so easy for The Major. Of course, he didn't believe any of that dribble. The important thing was that the other men believed every word. The Major believed that if he didn't take advantage of Stevens' vulnerability today, someone else would tomorrow. Stevens wasn't the kind of resource that lived long. Today, The Major would use Stevens and discard him without a second thought.

As soon as the truck disappeared up the gravel road, The Major took out his cell phone and noted the time. In fifteen minutes, he would open his app, enter his password, and re-activate the truck's GPS transponder, which the Army would pick up in seconds. And that was exactly what The Major wanted. He needed for the Army and/or the state police to detect the truck, to chase the truck, to catch the truck, to stop the truck, to swarm the truck, and to be consumed in the explosion. The authorities could waste hours if not days before they realized that there were no fragments of nuclear weapons at the detonation site.

Stevens would be the first of many necessary crew eliminations. The Major and his one real confidant, Flat Top, had no interest in starting a revolution or in restoring the Constitution. The Major didn't care about the slogans, the goals, the songs, the revolution, or any of the other pontifications that he had been spouting over the last few weeks. The Major and Flat Top only cared about stealing the two nukes and delivering them to their buyers in Los Angeles ten days from now.

Stevens would be the first to die. The others would follow. The Major had already arranged for the two stronger crewmembers to kill the two weaker crewmembers (Flea and Donny) to consolidate power to an inner circle of the strongest and most worthy members. Of course, once the inner circle eliminated Donny and Flea, The Major and Flat Top would eliminate the rest of the inner circle. In support of that plan, The Major emptied the clips in Donny's and Flea's pistols. He wanted to be certain that if either man were fast enough to mount a defense, the effort would be for naught. The Major also changed out the clips in the other two men's guns. He left five bullets in each of these clips -- just enough for them to eliminate Donny and Flea.

The other half of the Army for the Restoration of the Constitution was waiting in a warehouse in Oklahoma City. They believed that The Major, Flat Top, and the crew would bring the nuclear weapons to the warehouse and that they would all force politicians to revamp the government in compliance with the real intent of the Constitution. Of course, the Oklahoma City contingent was another diversion. The Major had instructed them to watch for signs that the authorities were onto their revolution. If the Oklahoma crew saw any indication that the authorities were moving in, they would carry out a public shootout with the police for as long as they could.

By procedure, the police would jam all phone service before assaulting the warehouse, so the crew couldn't call The Major and warn him away. The Major had told them that a public shootout with the police would be a headliner on every news channel. The newscast would warn The Major to stay away from Oklahoma City.

"If the authorities find you, fight for as long as you can," The Major had told them. "Your sacrifices will be remembered." Again, The Major didn't intend to remember anything. The Major had left a plethora of clues in the hunting cabin leading to the warehouse in Oklahoma City. If the authorities found the cabin, the evidence would lead them to the warehouse. A gun battle in Oklahoma City was a certainty. Again, while the inevitable gun battle raged, The Major and

Flat Top would be driving toward the west coast.

If the authorities captured anyone from the Oklahoma City brigade, no harm done. None of them knew any of the details of the real plan, anyway. The Oklahoma brigade was expendable, another diversion.

*****

Stevens and the deuce and a half passed out of sight around a bend in the driveway. When The Major turned to walk back into the barn, he came face-to-face with Flea. The Major neither liked nor disliked Flea. He did, however, flatter Flea at every turn to garner his cooperation and loyalty. But, as far as The Major was concerned, now that he had his weapons, Flea was nothing more than another functionless, expendable tool that he'd discard at the appropriate time.

"Flea," The Major called, "get a rag and a can of motor oil and start wiping down every surface that you can find. No fingerprints, right?"

"Yes, Sir," Flea answered with a snap in his voice.

"By the way, Flea, you did well today. History will remember you as a patriot who lived by his noble convictions."

As Flea set about his new assignment, The Major thought *so much for the butter and bullshit.* He remembered the first time he met Flea. It was a rabble-rousing meeting in a motel conference room. At that meeting, Flea was the sole new attendee. That made it easy for The Major to gauge Flea's reactions to his speech. The Major needed to know which parts of the rhetoric Flea agreed with and which parts he took umbrage with. So, as The Major spoke, he watched Flea's reaction to every sentence and ignored everyone else at the meeting.

For the attendees themselves, the meeting was about gathering national support to lobby the government to return to a purer form of their definition of a government's obligation to its citizens. For The Major and Flat Top, the meetings were a screening process designed to identify potential new members for The Major's real agenda: putting together the needed assets to steal a nuclear weapon or two.

The first part of the Major's message was benign, and most everyone who attended these meetings agreed with it. The message was that the Federal government was overstepping the definition of its charter in the Constitution of the United States; that our founding fathers designed the United States to be a republic, just as the Pledge of Allegiance states: "I pledge allegiance to the flag of the United States of America and to the Republic for which it stands..." The United States is a republican form of government, and in a republican form of government, matters of government should have been conducted at the lowest level of government possible, and our federal government was ignoring that mandate.

Flea agreed with this message. The Major saw Flea display positive body language, so he continued.

The second part of The Major's speech was a bit more controversial: he advocated that every citizen who wasn't satisfied with his government had a duty to let the government know of his dissatisfaction. Half of the attendees agreed that they, personally, should raise up their voices to the government. The other half believed that there was a legal way to challenge the government, but that they didn't know how to go about it.

The Major and Flat Top agreed later that Flea seemed to believe that he should act--so far so good.

The last part of The Major's presentation was the most controversial. The Major advocated, and history supported, the need for violent demonstrations of public opinion if the government wasn't heeding public outcry. The Major eloquently pointed out that American history supported such actions like The Boston Tea Party, the American Revolution, and, of course, freedom marches.

What The Major conveniently omitted was that the revolutionary Americans had no viable recourse except open revolt. Americans today had several functional alternatives to violence, including free speech, the vote, political recall, and referendum. The Major was adept at using only the facts that supported his agenda. He didn't want to be a part of an open rebellion; he just wanted to know who in his audience might be susceptible to the suggestion of open rebellion. Flea nodded his head in all the right places. He was a candidate for further cultivation.

Over the next few weeks, The Major and Flat Top cultivated Flea at every opportunity. They complimented him for every action and statement, agreed with him, and lauded him. They told Flea, "You're smart enough to understand our objectives. You should be in charge. You'll earn a place in the new order. We need you."

It was quite a con.

All the time that The Major and Flat Top were cultivating Flea's loyalty, they also learned what assets, abilities, and contacts Flea could bring to their scheme. The Major already had a welder and a milk truck driver. One of their numbers had access to an isolated, family-owned, hunting cabin. Another worked at a rollup door distributor, and another had a cheap source of contraband weapons. The Major kept collecting men and their assets until he had enough for a plan. When Flea joined their inner circle, The Major had the last resource he needed: a way to steal the nuclear weapons from Fort Sill. The Major and his financiers were happy.

*****

Duane was filling the napkin dispensers on the condiment counter when the phone by the cash register rang. He didn't think that it could be a client but gave the rehearsed greetings with enthusiasm, anyway, "Happy's Bait Shop."

"Hey, baby," Cindy's voice was soothing and inviting as always.

"Hey, Cindy. You still at work?"

"Yeah, Cheryl came in early tonight. I'm on my way home. Any chance you could leave early?"

"That's good news. I will if I can. I can't wait to see you."

"Make sure you come in quiet. I don't want to wake my parents."

"Watch for me. Love you."

"Love you, too. Hurry. "Bye."

*****

As soon as The Major stopped to talk to Stevens, Flat Top stepped back from where he was supervising the milk truck loading. He watched the exchange between the two at the side of the deuce and a half. Flat Top was sure that he knew all the details of their scheme, but, always cautious, he took note of any interactions between The Major and a member of the crew. The Major was as close a friend or partner as Flat Top ever had. Still, Flat Top didn't totally trust him. He knew how devious The Major could be. He also knew how many blindsides and double crosses were built into the next few hours. He knew what The Major planned for Stevens. He knew what The Major had planned for the rest of the crew. Flat Top was vigilant to ensure that The Major didn't have any plot twists planned for him.

Flat Top considered himself a superior human being in every way. He was taller and stronger than most. He had two years of college and a broad paramilitary education even though he had not personally served in the armed forces. He was also able to remain detached from human emotion or empathy when using the people around him. As far as Flat Top was concerned, he could do anything he wanted without any of the regrets or consequences that plagued most people. Flat Top believed this gave Flat Top an advantage. The average person was on Earth to serve Flat Top, and when his use for them ended, he'd discard them as easily as used coffee grounds.

Flat Top watched the short meeting with a smug sneer of insight as to what The Major was doing. The Major was exercising the very trait that allowed Flat Top to tolerate him: he was coldly using another person for his own purposes. The ability to use this white trash without encumbering emotions defined their superiority. Flat Top enjoyed watching The Major work. He did have a gift for words.

As Stevens stepped away from The Major and headed for the truck, Flat Top almost laughed aloud at the stupid look of hero worship on Stevens' face.

You poor, dumb schmuck. Go and die.

Stevens disappeared around the side of the truck, and Flat Top's gaze drifted to The Major's face. He didn't like what he saw: The Major's face had softened for an instant in empathy. Flat Top knew that The Major was hard as nails and that he would do whatever was necessary, or use whomever he had to, to complete the job. However, in unprotected moments, The Major let his soft, useless, feminine side express itself. The Major had a weakness. He cared, occasionally. The Major's rare surrender to emotion was what assured Flat Top that he was superior even to The Major. He lived by the belief that he couldn't trust any man who gave in to pity. One could never be sure when the trait would exert itself.

Chapter Sixteen

Cassie ran at an easy pace and thought about what she would do when she reached the highway. She couldn't leave the mouth of the driveway to get help; the men might leave in the milk truck while she was away. If they left, Cassie had to somehow get on board, or at least see which direction they went. She wondered if it was wise to sit on the side of the road and wait for a passerby at midnight in the Oklahoma countryside.

A flash of light illuminated the exposed sand and grasses to Cassie's left and then faded. Cassie's night vision was overwhelmed. When the light was gone, she was night blind. At the same moment, Cassie recognized the rumble of a big truck engine. Without thinking, she dove into the grasses to her right and got prone. She blinked a couple of times to regain her vision. The deuce and a half passed within inches of her.

With an instinct born from training, Cassie sprang up and took two quick steps to the passenger side of the truck. She put one foot on the running board and grabbed the lowest mirror support strut. Without pulling herself above the bottom of the passenger window, she brought her other foot up onto the running board.

Cassie counted her lucky stars, she didn't have to run all the way to the highway, but she couldn't let the deuce and a half with a bomb on board leave the area. She didn't even consider diving through the passenger window, wrestling the gun away from the driver, beating him unconscious with one hand, and shoving his unconscious body out the driver's door with the other. That sort of theatrics was only successful in the movies. Besides, if the driver eliminated her now, there would be no one to guide the authorities to the milk truck and the nukes. Cassie had to know beyond a shadow of doubt that she would prevail if she were to engage this driver. She was conflicted. She still wanted to neutralize this bomb threat.

Cassie assumed that the driver had his pistol lying on the seat next to him. She had to separate the pistol from the man if she were to have a chance to take him out. If she could disarm him, she was confident that her hand-to-hand combat training would give her the advantage. If she couldn't, she might have to let him go and trust that others could stop him before he detonated his bomb. Even though the bomb was small compared to the bomb that devastated Oklahoma City in 1995, it could still hurt a lot of people.

*****

Stevens slowed the truck as he approached the highway. He felt like he might throw up at any moment. He didn't like being alone to perform this phase of the operation. He didn't like being away from the constant support of Flat Top and The Major. Stevens tried not to admit the truth, but he was scared sick. At the stop sign, he stopped the truck, put it in neutral, set the brake, opened the door, leaned out as far as he could, and puked. He hoped that no one would ever find out that he lost it. He didn't want to feel small. No, Stevens didn't like being alone.

*****

Cassie was still weighing her options when the truck reached the highway and stopped. Cassie stepped down and started to take her first step into the brush, but she heard the driver's door open. He was getting out. She froze. He might not have his weapon with him. This might be her opportunity. She crouched to look under the truck and see which way he would go, but the driver's boots never hit the ground. Cassie took a chance and moved around to the front of the truck, keeping as low as she could. When she got in front of the grill, the driver had still not gotten out of the truck. She listened as the driver gurgled and retched. Apparently, his fear was getting the better of him. He leaned out of the cab of the truck and threw up. She imagined that she could smell the acrid odor. She was confident that he didn't have his gun. *Who remembers to pick up a gun when they're heaving?* The open truck door would block his field of vision as she rushed him. She tensed for the dash around the truck.

The door slammed shut and the truck lurched forward, catching Cassie with both feet planted on the ground and her body bent over. The impact knocked Cassie sideways. She twisted in the air and landed on her butt, legs straight, facing the truck. She was below the driver's line of sight, and the truck was coming fast. Cassie flopped to the ground like a fish and turned the toes of her boots to the side to present as low a profile as possible. She landed on the hard packed dirt and not on the pavement, but her shoulders hit hard, and her head hit harder. She saw a flash of white light behind her eyelids. Bits of gravel gouged into her scalp and flecks of the dust landed in her eyes. She tried to squint them away.

The truck's high undercarriage passed inches above Cassie. She could smell the truck's hot engine mixed with the dirt. The left rear tire brushed her left shoulder and smeared dirt on her shirt. If the driver had turned more sharply, the wheel would have rolled over Cassie's arm. As soon as the truck's rear bumper passed over her, she rolled off the dirt and into the grass.

Cassie checked her shoulder and found nothing but an angry scrape. She lay face down with her nose on the ground, waiting for the adrenaline spike to fade. She blinked to clear her eyes. Even though she was still trembling, she looked up to see the deuce and a half heading west, possibly north, on… whatever highway this was. She brushed at the back of her head to remove the dirt and pulled her hand back to see a half-inch wide smear of blood. The head laceration couldn't have been very bad or there would have been more blood. Cassie put her head back down and just breathed. The situation kept changing. It was time to go back to her original plan.

*****

Stevens turned the truck onto the highway and started to accelerate. He felt better now, braver. He looked at the gun and trigger lying on the seat next to him. Their presence bolstered him even more. He was still afraid, but not to the point of being sick. His biggest fear now was disappointing The Major.

The Major and Flat Top had always treated him well. They listened to his opinions and considered his council. They told him about their plans and explained the reasons behind their orders. Not many people bothered to explain things to Stevens; they just ordered him around like he was incapable of adult reasoning. Stevens didn't like it when people treated him that way, but he didn't know how to stop it. With The Major, he didn't have to try and figure out how to stop bad treatment. With The Major, there wasn't any bad treatment.

Stevens was convinced that The Major saw real potential in him. He always talked about Stevens' place in the new government. Stevens felt valued, understood, capable, and he liked it. Tonight, he was afraid of making a mistake. But The Major had faith in him, which helped him have faith in himself. He drove west as The Major told him, determined to make The Major proud.

*****

Cassie moved twenty yards up the highway. She couldn't just stop any car on the road. If she stopped the wrong vehicle, the driver might be part of the gang at the cabin. No, Cassie had to wait to be sure that the driver wasn't going to turn into the driveway. If a car came from her left, it would pass Cassie before it could pass the driveway, and if the vehicle kept going, Cassie would be unable to catch it and the opportunity would be lost. She had to wait for a vehicle coming from her right. She guessed that Fort Sill and Lake Lawtonka were to the right. If the vehicle drove past the driveway, she could flag it down.

*****

It was almost midnight before Duane finished his cleanup. He never quite got around to all the straightening and cleaning that he planned, but he made enough significant improvements to the bait shop that he knew Max would be pleased. He stowed his rags and cleaning supplies, grabbed the two big bags of trash, walked to the front door, and paused.

Letting the door close behind him was an irreversible step. Once out, he couldn't get back in. So, out of habit he turned around and surveyed the room. It was a good thing that he did, because his schoolbag was sitting on one of the stools at the narrow bar that ran along the front windows. A few nights earlier, he found that he had left a can of bug spray on the floor by the soft drink cooler. Duane walked back in and slung his bag over his shoulder. Again, he headed for the door, and again, he surveyed the room. This time, he was satisfied with what he saw. He stepped out and let the shop's door close behind him. He tossed the evening's trash in the dumpster.

With a fleeting prayer that his truck would start, he got into the beast. Since he was anxious to get to Cindy's for the evening, he figured the truck would be troublesome. He cranked the truck twice to no avail. On the third try, it kicked over. *Nice.* Duane turned his headlights toward Cindy's parents' house on Highway 49.

Duane had mixed feelings about driving the back roads of Oklahoma in the middle of the night. He was alone and there weren't many signs of development or civilization. On several occasions, Duane imagined that he was alone in this quiet world and that he owned all that he could see. At times, he appreciated that his life was quiet enough for him to concentrate on his education and surviving another day. At other times, his life was so quiet that he feared he'd lose his direction out of sheer boredom. He craved a little excitement once and a while.

His relationship with Cindy was the one bit of excitement in his life. She was part of every thought he had and every action that he took. Every plan that he made included Cindy. He recognized at the start of their relationship that his life was going to be better with Cindy in it. He thought she was one of the most naturally intelligent people that he had ever met. She had little formal education and didn't believe that her limited education would take her anywhere. Cindy had few people in her life who recognized her abilities and encouraged her to develop her natural people skills.

More importantly, Cindy made him feel like he was somebody and that his opinion mattered. She understood him. Cindy explained the world to Duane in words and examples that he understood. Duane valued her explanations so much that he played a mental game with himself. He imagined that Cindy was standing next to him all the time. *Would she have a better way of wording my next statement or question? Would she think that my next action was relevant and necessary? Would she be embarrassed by my actions?*

Duane was convinced that Cindy had saved his life and would continue to save his life. What Duane didn't know was that Cindy felt the same way about Duane. Cindy appreciated the strength of Duane's character and his confidence. She had received little encouragement as a child. Her parents weren't neglectful or overly negative; they just didn't see the value of believing in *unreachable* goals. As a result, Cindy didn't believe in herself or in her inherent intelligence. Duane took the time to compliment Cindy's good decisions and clear thinking. He always commented on the good results that came from her natural win-win point of view. He had a way of making her realize the value of her natural abilities.

Together, they were the perfect pair. Each possessed the skills and talents that the other lacked and realized that a growing relationship with the other was in both of their best interests. Both were convinced that the other was in this world to save them.

Duane was daydreaming about his evening with Cindy when something jumped out in front of the truck.

"Ahhh!" Duane stomped the brakes and turned the steering wheel out of the way of, what, a deer? *Stupid thing. One car within twenty miles and this moron has to jump out in front of me. What the hell are those? Asterisks?*

The objects in his headlights weren't asterisks; they were hands. They were chalk white human hands, fingers splayed, palms facing him. They looked like two giant asterisks lit up by the truck's headlights. That was a person out there, not a deer.

Duane looked a second time and saw a girl wearing tan digital military pants, work shirt, and combat boots. Duane's truck hadn't come to a complete stop before the girl was at the driver's window.

"My name is Lance Corporal Cassandra Sing, United States Marine Corps. I am evoking the Patriot Act of September 2001 and declaring a matter of national security. Give me your cell phone!"

Startled, Duane dutifully handed Cassie his cell phone and mumbled something about the battery being dead and that he didn't have a car charger.

Cassie handed him his phone and eyed the rifle in the gun rack behind him.

"I need your rifle. Do you have any extra ammunition?"

Duane shrugged and smiled, "Sorry, the rifle's broken and I don't have any bullets."

Cassie frowned and looked down the road for inspiration. Without a weapon, she couldn't confront the men. And no, she couldn't go for help. The men might get away or, worse, the men might get away with the nuclear weapons. Cassie had to stay. She had to trust this civilian to call in the alarm and a request for backup. She turned back to Duane.

"I need your help. Again, this is a matter of national security. I need you to alert the authorities of my situation, and to request some military backup at this location. Do you have a pencil and paper?" Even as she asked, she knew that few people carried pencil and paper with them.

Duane held up his book bag and said, "I do. I just got out of class."

He opened his bag and gave Cassie a pen and essay tablet. As Cassie started to write, Duane asked, "Who are you? What's going on? Are we in any danger?" Duane was becoming uneasy and surveyed the open desert around him.

"As I said, my name is Lance..." Cassie saw his concern and softened. "My name is Cassie. I need you to deliver this message to military police at the Fort Sill north gate. I can't leave this area. You'll have to hurry. I don't know how much longer my situation will be stable."

Cassie handed Duane the note. "Read it back to me."

Duane took the tablet and read aloud, "My name is Lance Corporal Cassandra Sing, USMC. At dusk this evening, I witnessed the murder of two MPs at the Fort Sill north gate. I have eyes on the perpetrators. I also have eyes on two stolen nuclear weapons, type unknown." Duane gave Cassie a wide-eyed look and repeated "nuclear weapons" with stunned emphasis, and added, "Are you kidding me?" He continued to read, "I am unarmed and have no means of communication. I am in critical need of armed backup. Caution! Do not approach stolen deuce and a half. Truck contains a 150-gallon fertilizer bomb. Driver is a suicide bomber. Repeat: do not approach stolen deuce and a half. It's a trap. Caller can give you my location, cabin, and outbuilding. Nukes hidden in modified milk tanker truck. Do not let milk truck leave the area. Do not approach the deuce and a half."

Cassie nodded, "Good. What road are we on?"

"Highway 49."

"How far are we from Fort Sill?"

"Thirty-five, maybe forty minutes."

She nodded again, "Good, is there a phone available nearby?"

"Not that I can think of. This is pretty desolate country." Duane looked around.

"Can you find this driveway again?"

"Sure."

"Drive toward Fort Sill to the nearest mile marker and write the number down on the last line of the note. There will be a large MP presence at the Fort Sill north gate. Bring the MPs back here. The nukes and the men who stole them are at a small hunting cabin about three quarters of a mile up that dirt road. There's a large pole barn and an over-sized gravel parking lot. The men have silenced automatic pistols. You must be as fast as possible. My life and the lives of many others hang in the balance. Go now!"

Duane started to put his truck into gear but called out the window, "Where will you be?"

"I'm going back to the cabin. If you don't get back in time, I'll try to stop them or, at least, slow them down. Get going. Wait, what time is it?"

"It's twelve-thirty in the morning."

Duane watched Cassie wave an acknowledgement over her shoulder and then trot back to the mouth of the driveway.

"Tell them that a female Marine 'friendly' is on site and ask them not to shoot me." With that, Cassie disappeared into the darkness.

Duane decided that he wouldn't drive the thirty-some miles to Fort Sill. He had a better idea.

Fort Sill was forty-five minutes on these back roads. The nearest phone he knew of was at the bait shop, but the bait shop was locked. He considered breaking in, but a better plan came to him. Cindy's house was less than fifteen minutes from there, and she had several working phones at her house. He could call Fort Sill faster than he could drive there and would have less distance to drive back to the site to show the MPs where the mouth of the dirt road was.

He turned toward Cindy's house, away from Fort Sill. He couldn't wait to tell Cindy about the two stolen nuclear weapons. He had driven a whooping three tenths of a mile when he saw mile marker 152. That meant the dirt road was at mile marker 151 and seven tenths. He was writing the mileage down on Lance Corporal Sing's note when his truck gave up all pretenses of cooperation and died. It didn't sputter, wheeze, or clank. It just died.

As Duane guided the truck to the side of the road, he thanked whatever guardian angel made him decide to go to Cindy's instead of Fort Sill. If he had headed for Fort Sill, he would have been twenty country miles from the nearest help on a road with no traffic. As it was, he was less than five miles from Cindy's. He could run to Cindy's from where the truck died; well, he could alternately run and walk to Cindy's house.

He took his backpack and notebook, locked his truck, and started jogging.

Chapter Seventeen

Cassie felt better now that she had called in reinforcements. She made a quick calculation. It was forty-five minutes to Fort Sill and forty-five minutes back, and it was twelve thirty now. She could expect the troops to arrive no later than two a.m.

Cassie again ran with an easy gait. As she ran, Cassie absent-mindedly hummed a Marine Corps running cadence:

I packed my trash and headed for the planes.

I went to a place where they made Marines.

Oh Yeah!

Oh Yeah!

Paris Island was the name of the place.

The first thing I saw was the drill in-structor's face.

Oh Yeah!

Oh Yeah!

He had razor cuts and a Smokey Bear.

Mountain climbing privates were eve-rywhere.

Oh Yeah!

Oh Yeah!

Humming the cadence made the running easier. It also brought back memories of recruit training and the Marine Corps Recruit Depot, Paris Island.

*****

For Recruit Sing, the rumors and stories about the Chemical Weapons Training Center (the gas chamber) were the most unsettling. The gas chamber was a sealed, one-room, cinder block bunker of a building on the far western edge of the training field. The Marines used a non-lethal form of Chlorobenzylidene Malornitrile (CBM) in the gas chamber. CBM would form an opaque haze in the chamber to make visibility difficult even with a functioning gas mask. The limited visibility was the reason that the drill instructors took the recruits into the chamber in groups of twenty or so. CBM was a debilitating but survivable experience.

Recruit Sing's Recruit Training Company could see the gas chamber from most of the other training venues every day. Recruits Sing's company could also see the recruits in earlier training rotations entering and leaving the gas chamber. Sometimes, they could hear the recruits coughing, gagging, and puking. Some of the recruits fell to their hands and knees. Other recruits were walking in circles with their arms outstretched to prevent hotspots from burning, waiting for the pain to subside.

The day that recruit Sings company had gas chamber training started out like any other day: up at 4:00 a.m., chow by five, an hour of calisthenics, and a five-mile run. After the recruits reached the training venue, they formed up, facing the gas chamber and stood at ease. Sixty seconds later, two male, specialized training instructors emerged from the gas chamber. Both removed their gas masks.

The first instructor stepped up onto a four-foot square platform and started his monologue.

"Good morning, my name is Staff Sergeant Dominique. This morning, you will gain experience using your chemical weapons protective mask by entering the gas chamber. The gas we use is a non-lethal form of CBM. We've never lost a recruit in this training exercise. If anyone has any sinus stuffiness, we will eliminate those symptoms for you today."

Recruit Sing thought, *there's a lethal form of CBM?*

"In groups of twenty, you enter the gas chamber with your gas mask in your right hand. As soon as you gag or cough one time, you put your gas masks on and make the necessary adjustments. As soon as you have fitted your mask, you will take several rapid, deep breaths to clear your mask of noxious chemicals. You will be able to breathe. When your breathing returns to normal, raise your hand. When the instructor points to you, you will walk to the exit. You will remove your mask and state your name, rank, and serial number. When the instructor is satisfied, he will signal for you to leave the gas chamber. You will exit the gas chamber with dignity and discipline. You will not drop your gas mask. If you do, you will re-enter the chamber, retrieve the mask, and re-peat the exercise. Do you understand? Any questions?"

The instructor pointed to the front ranks of the Alpha Recruit Company and said, "First twenty recruits, front and center."

Recruit Sing was in Bravo Company, so she had to watch several groups of recruits enter the chamber. She was more than a little anxious.

After too short a time, the drill in-structor called Recruit Sing's group. She lined up with the other recruits. The drill in-structor at the door admitted recruits one at a time. As soon as each recruit coughed once, the drill instructor at the door pushed her further into the room and ordered her to put on her mask.

"Next!"

Recruit Sing stepped through the door. The gas chamber was a steam bath from hell. A heavy chemical fog hung in the room. The fog was hot. Recruit Sing could see the four walls of the room, but just barely. A heavy residue of CBM gas from previous sessions coated the windows. They were dirty with years of grime. Before Recruit Sing could take a breath, the gas started to burn her eyes. The moist inner surface of her nose reacted to the burning assault. Her nose started to run, trying to eliminate the noxious invader. The sweat on the hot spots of her skin catalyzed the effectiveness of the gas. Every crease in her skin and every hot spot felt as though she had horrible sunburn.

A drill instructor stepped up next to her. *My god,* she thought, *these DIs stay in here for the whole session. How do they stand it? Extended exposure must have some lasting effects.*

"Name!" the drill instructor demanded from inside her mask. Her voice was muffled and indistinct. She sounded more

like Darth Vader than a Marine drill instructor.

Out of an abundance of training and
repeated usage, Recruit Sing snapped to attention and shouted, or tried to shout, "Recruit Sing, Cassandra, Drill Instructor!"

Unfortunately, for Recruit Sing, her
body's first impulse was to take a quick,
deep breath to maximize the volume of her
response. When the gas hit her throat and
lungs, her body reacted by taking the deepest
breath possible to facilitate the deepest cough
to expel the poison she was breathing. Recruit Sing didn't complete the word "recruit"
before the spasm seized her chest.

The training drill instructor shouted,
"Mask, now!"

Recruit Sing couldn't think. Her brain
had no practiced response to choking on gas.
She couldn't see through the acid tears in her
eyes. She couldn't think past the sensation of
burning embers on her skin. Cassie's trained
response to following orders saved her. Her
training commanded her body to place the
mask over her head and down onto her face.
She hoped that she wouldn't puke in the
mask. When Recruit Sing reached for the ad-
justing straps, the drill instructor nudged Recruit Sing further into the room. Out of habit,

the drill instructor checked for downed rec-ruits. The floor was clear.

Recruit Sing finished fitting the gas mask. Within a couple of breaths, she was aware that her repeated breaths were clearing the air in the mask and her gag reflex was relaxing. She still couldn't see anything through her tears, especially in the dim light. She could hear the other recruits fighting to control their breathing. The oppressive heat was making her sweat, which increased the effectiveness of the gas.

From somewhere far away in the fog, a Darth Vader voice ordered, "Approach the door one at a time. Remove your mask. State your name, rank, and serial number. When you have said it correctly, I will let you leave the building."

Recruit Sing hung back a moment and let some of the other recruits step to the door first. She didn't want to appear too ea-ger or too panicked. She could breathe, somewhat. She knew that the burning on her skin would go away in the first few minutes after leaving the gas chamber. She also wan-ted to leave the impression that she was a tough bad ass.

At her turn, Cassie stepped up to the door, took a deep breath, removed her mask, and started to recite the required words. Even though she took a deep breath before taking off her gas mask, habit forced her to take a small breath before starting to speak. She gagged and coughed as she said her last name. To complete the lengthy identification took two breaths. She willed herself to keep speaking. Her lungs were burning much worse now. She wasn't sure that her words were intelligible, but she completed the test. The drill instructor tapped her on the shoulder and released her from the building. Recruit Sing's efforts paid off for her. She didn't have to repeat the citation. Some of the recruits had to say everything twice, and a few had to try a third time.

Once outside, Recruits Sing's first noticeable relief came with the cool afternoon air. Instantly, her skin felt soothed. She joined the group of recruits who looked like they were playing airplane and walking in a large circle trying to clear themselves of the debilitating effects of the gas. Others were on their hands and knees. Some were puking. Recruit Sing followed the recruit in front of her, one step at a time. She kept her arms out like an airplane. Her first impulse was to wipe her face and neck with her hands, but from the classroom training, she remembered that any touch to her skin while the gas was still present heightened the burning effect.

Recruit Sing bent over at the waist and continued walking. She didn't want the tears from her eyes, the mucus from her nose, or the spittle from her mouth to drip onto her clothes. She fought hard not to fall to her knees or to puke. It was a matter of pride. She repeated to herself, *just keep walking, deep breath, deep breath. It'll be over in a minute. It'll be over in a minute, deep breath, deep breath.*

And it was over in minutes. The Marine Corps didn't aerate mineral oil into the gas mixture for recruit training. The oil free gas dissipated quickly because there was nothing to bind it to the skin or the inside of the nose, throat, or lungs. If the drill instructor had mixed a drop of mineral oil into the gas mixture before atomizing it, the gas would bind to any contact surfaces. The recovery time for exposure to gas infused with oil was excruciating longer and more difficult.

Fifteen minutes after walking out of the gas chamber, Recruit Sing's breathing was relaxed and nearly normal. The burning on her skin was gone, and her eyes were clear. She left the recovery circle and joined the ranks of other recovered recruits. Fifteen minutes later, the last of the recruits left the circle and joined the ranks.

"Fall in! Listen up! We designed the gas chamber exercise with two objectives in mind. The first is to instill in you a confidence that the chemical weapons protective mask is effective. It will save your life if you trust it to do its job. The second objective was to demonstrate that the anticipation of a difficult event is usually worse than the experience of the event itself. We know that you recruits had a measure of concern for the obvious pain and discomfort of chemical weapons training. All of you have successfully completed the training. Don't let your fears control your actions."

The sound of two companies of female recruit's double-timing down the adjacent road singing a loud and proud cadence interrupted the drill instructor's speech.

The drill instructor shouted, "Companies, be at ease! Turn and pay your respects to the Marine Corps' two newest companies of Marines. They have just completed the Crucible. You will face the Crucible in five weeks. Pray you perform as well as those Marines. Many recruits don't complete the Crucible. Companies, fall in!"

"Drill instructors, front and center. Company, right… face. Forward… march."

As they left the gas chamber training arena, Recruit Sing had several thoughts.

They were right. It wasn't as bad as I imagined.

She wouldn't have missed the training exercise for all the tea in China. She also wouldn't voluntarily go through it again for all the *gold* in China. As they marched, Cassie watched the two companies of new Marines disappear into the distance. They seemed so strong and energetic. Cassie wondered if the Crucible was as difficult as everyone said. She turned her attention back to the here-and-now. Her two companies of recruits continued their march back to their barracks and evening chow. Recruit Sing stole a look over the rest of the training venues and the recruits who were there. She wondered how many of them were looking at her company and imagining the worst of the gas chamber training.

*****

Cassie stepped off the driveway and into the desert before it turned into the gravel parking lot. She skirted to the left around the cabin and, once again, entered the open space between the piles of debris. She found a small nook in one of the piles and settled in to keep watch over her theater of operation. She had met her main goal to get reinforcements when she met Duane. While she watched, she tried to solve her other two goals: to stop the milk truck from leaving the area and to guarantee the capture of the men.

Every now and then, one or two of the men would walk to the cabin, stay a few minutes, and then walk back to the barn. The parked vehicles caught her attention once again. She knew that it was too risky to try to disable the vehicles, but, as she stared at the pickup trucks, she realized she had a fallback option.

She pulled a wooden plank from one of the debris piles and scratched her name and rank into the weathered wood. She berated herself for not asking Duane for an extra piece of paper and a pencil. She scratched each letter down to virgin wood and was satisfied with the way the letters stood out. Below her name, she scratched "vehicles present." She finished the message by scratching the license plate numbers from the three vehicles into the wood. She arranged stones into a makeshift easel and set the plank on them. Against the background of the original debris piles, the plank stood out like a movie marquee.

Hopefully, Cassie could prevent the men from leaving. If not, the plank provided a clue to their identities.

For the milk truck, Cassie's best plan was to wait until all the men were out of the barn, sneak into the barn, disable the truck, withdraw into the desert, and wait for the cavalry to arrive. She just wasn't sure just how she was going to disable the truck. She doubted she had enough strength to puncture the oil pan or radiator. She thought about letting the air out of the tires, but the men would just re-inflate the tires and look for an intruder. She thought about poking some holes in the back tires, but commercial truck tires were tough, and she wasn't sure if it was worth the risk to try. For now, all she could do was watch.

Cassie let a deep sigh escape. She was getting tired.

Cassie froze. There was a slight shift in shadows by the next debris pile. As she was searching for the cause, another field mouse hopped into view. Maybe, it was the same mouse. It was a few feet from Cassie's boots. It turned and looked at Cassie but didn't run away.

Conspirators meet in the night.

Cassie moved one of her boots an inch and the mouse darted away.

"Yeah, run away," Cassie said quietly. The soft sound of her own voice made her feel less alone.

"I'd run away, too, if I could, but I'm committed."

Cassie rose up on her haunches and surveyed the driveway, looking for her reinforcements.

"It's been too long," she said to the night. "I'm not sure that the cowboy did as I asked. They may not be coming."

She sat back into her niche.

"I may be out here all alone, not a happy thought.

"I always knew that I might have to stand a post on a wall somewhere, some time. I just didn't think that I'd be standing on it alone. But then, it only takes one Marine, right?" She chuckled to herself. The words were relaxing her.

"I mean, I could just spring up and demand that they surrender," Cassie grinned.

"I always thought my wall would be in some far away, exotic land in the far distant future. What do I do, now?'

Chapter Eighteen

Duane jogged the last hundred yards to Cindy's house. His legs were like wobbly, wet noodles, but he kept thinking about why he wasn't allowing himself to slow down: two nuclear weapons.

Duane trotted past the mailbox with the Mathews name on top of it, up the drive-way, and around the side of the house. The property had no fences, so he had a clear shot to the backyard. Cindy's parents had bought this house for one unique feature: a private mother-in-law entrance on the back of the house. A long hall ran down the middle of the house from front to back. The family room, formal living room, dining room, and kitchen were on the left, and the four bed-rooms and two bathrooms were on the right. The kitchen and family room opened to the hall, but not the formal living room or dining room. There was an entrance from the kit-chen into the back yard, and one from the laundry room. The mother-in-law entrance opened from the hallway to the patio.

In effect, the back bedroom and bath-room was a separate apartment with a private entrance and an access to the kitchen. The other guest bathroom separated the master suite in the front of the house from the rest of the bedrooms. When Cindy moved home, the mother-in-law suite became the adult-daughter-moved-home suite.

Duane stepped up to Cindy's bed-room window, tapped on the glass with the tips of two fingers, and then stepped around to the private entrance. Cindy must have been awake because she opened the door at once. She pressed her finger to his lips to shush him. After she closed her bedroom door, she slapped him on the shoulder and chastised him in a low, playful voice.

"Where have you been? I've been worried sick. Why didn't you answer your phone?" Then, making fun of him, she added, "Did your truck break down, again?"

Duane put his finger on Cindy's lips to stop the flow of words, then gave her a peck on the lips, "Yes, my truck broke down. But something happened tonight. I'll explain in a few minutes. Right now, I need your cell phone and for you to get dressed. I need for you to drive me back out to the highway."

"I'm not going back out tonight. Are you deluded? It's two thirty in the morning."

Duane looked at his watch for the hundredth time. It was two thirty. The girl in the desert was expecting reinforcements half an hour ago.

"Cindy," he said a little more sharply, "I'll explain when we're on the road. Give me your cell phone and get dressed. The girl who stopped me said, 'Patriot Act, Homeland Security, two MPs killed, and two stolen nukes.' Now, get your phone for me and get dressed please."

Cindy froze for a second, her face expressionless. She knew from his expression that the situation was serious. She walked to her nightstand, unplugged her cell phone, handed it to Duane, and started to get dressed.

She asked, "What girl?"

Duane ignored Cindy's question as he dialed 411. When the operator came on Duane asked, "Fort Sill Military Police, the Operations Desk, please."

Cindy listened as she dressed faster. Duane was calling the military police. Five minutes later, Duane had finished the phone report and arranged to meet the military police on Highway 49 at mile marker 151 and seven tenths. As he and Cindy walked to Cindy's car, he told her the whole story from the flash of Cassie's hands in his headlights to his running to her house.

*****

At the Military Police Headquarters, the duty officer was still busy transitioning the base out of the Lockdown status when an NCO stepped to his side, "Sir, we received this phone call from a civilian named Duane Conners. You'd better take a listen."

The duty officer took the earpiece and listened to the call. As it played, he bowed his head and stared at a spot on the floor. Without looking up he said, "Play it again."

"You think it's legit?"

"He knew the name of our missing Marine and that we've lost two nukes. I'd say it's a hundred percent."

"Re-direct our ground teams to mile marker 151 on Highway 49. Call the Air Cav and release those two Black Hawks for a hostage and weapons recovery operation. Send both a copy of that recording. Both are weapons hot but caution them that we're in the states: selective weapons use only.

He addressed the command center, "Okay, everybody, listen up. Play the tape." After the tape played, he added, "We're shifting our focus to hostage and weapons recovery. Continue to re-open the base. Dean, get me a topographical map of the area around mile marker 151. Everybody, go to work."

*****

At 3:55 a.m., Cassie was still watching the scene unfold around her. Most of the men stayed in the pole barn, and some continued to walk to the cabin and back. Sometimes, they carried more junk food and drinks, and sometimes they returned empty handed. *Potty breaks?*

Cassie's reinforcements were late. She wondered if something had gone wrong with Duane. On the other hand, the longer that the situation remained quiet, the better the chances would be that reinforcements would arrive.

Suddenly, Cassie's wait was over. The rollup door at the end of the pole barn rose, bathing the desert in bright light. The once muted music got decibels louder, and Cassie could now read the men's lips. She rolled onto her side to get a better look. Someone started the milk truck's engine.

Two of the men walked out of the pole barn and seemed to walk straight toward her, but it was an illusion. The men were walking their usual path to the cabin. Before they entered, another man came out of the barn and stood just outside the open door. One of the men went into the cabin and came back out with a box. He put the box in the back of the newer truck, then went to the cabin again.

Cassie looked back to the barn. The milk truck's engine was still warming up. With the men entering and leaving the parking area from both sides, Cassie couldn't move. The situation forced her to sit tight and wait. *Where were her reinforcements*? She needed them now.

Cassie had only one viable option. If the men tried to move the milk truck, she could run out into the open and cause a ruckus. She hoped the men would chase her and try to capture her. She would run off into the desert and lead them on as long a chase as she could. She decided that the extra few minutes' delay was worth the risk. Cassie watched and waited as she tried to come up with a better plan. The constant stress and state of readiness were beginning to make Cassie feel a little strung out.

*****

It took Cindy ten minutes to drive back out to mile marker 151, passing Duane's truck on the way. Duane insisted that Cindy park her car astride the double yellow lines in front of the driveway. Cindy started to object but that there wasn't much chance of another vehicle on the Highway at this time of night. Besides, Duane wanted to make sure that the military police would see them.

"Is this the spot?" Cindy asked. "Is this where she jumped out of the brush?" Cindy scanned the area for any signs of life.

"This is it. She jumped out right there as I came around that curve up there," Duane said, pointing to a spot at the side of the road.

"There?" Cindy asked, pointing to the same spot. "Wow, jumping out on your blind side. She's lucky you didn't run her down."

"I damn near did. That's where she disappeared back into the desert, over there."

Cindy asked, "Okay, where are the military police? Let's get this show on the road."

"They'll be here any minute," Duane said absentmindedly.

Duane and Cindy leaned against the front hood of Cindy's car, waiting. The night was cool. They were alone (as Duane often fantasized, alone in the world). Far in the distance, a coyote howled his discontent. The night seemed to grow darker, more concealing, and Cindy wondered what Duane would do if she reached over and kissed him right now. She decided to find out. She raised her eyes to the road in front of her, and, before she could turn her gaze to Duane, the glow of headlights lit the turn in the road ahead of them.

Cindy and Duane stood up. A jeep raced around the turn. In an instant, two more followed. The lead jeep seemed intent on hitting them. He wasn't slowing down. Cindy took a defensive step behind Duane.

Before the lead jeep reached Cindy's car, the third jeep in the line screeched to a halt, turned a one-eighty, and sped back to the turn in the road. Duane saw the jeep's brake lights through the brush as it stopped across the lanes just around the bend. Even though Cindy's car was sitting astride the middle line of the highway, the first jeep passed Duane and Cindy at full speed and stopped just beyond their line of sight on the turn behind them. Duane and Cindy didn't see the MPs from both jeeps set up barriers across both lanes, isolating the little stretch of the highway.

Sorry for the inconvenience. This section of road is closed. An Army septic pumping truck dumped part of its load on the road ahead. You'll have to go around on State Route 62 and up Route 54. The road should be open by morning. Sorry for the inconvenience, folks. Move along, please.

The middle jeep stopped fifty feet from Duane and Cindy and bathed them in white, high-intensity floodlights. Neither Duane nor Cindy could see the jeep in the glare, but they could see the silhouette of the MPs who jumped out either side and pointed their rifles at Duane and Cindy. Duane threw his hands into the air. Cindy stood frozen, wide-eyed.

A soldier, hidden by the glare of the search lights, keyed his public address system, and ordered, "Hands up, palms open! Female move out from behind the male and take three steps to your right."

Cindy did as he instructed.

"Both of you take ten steps forward away from the vehicle!"

As Duane and Cindy walked forward, a silhouetted shadow detached itself from the glare surrounding the jeep and circled around behind them. The soldier carried what Duane thought was an antique video camera or radio.

"Eyes front, feet apart!" A second silhouette walked toward Duane and Cindy. "Male subject, state your name and place of birth."

"Duane Connors, Albuquerque, New Mexico," Duane answered.

The soldier patted them down, then stepped back, satisfied they weren't armed. Duane could see at least one more silhouette by the jeep with a rifle pointed at him.

The soldier that ran to Cindy's car called out from behind Duane, "Vehicle's clear."

The soldier in front of Duane relaxed and ordered, "State your reason for being here."

"Corporal Sing told me to call you and then come back here and show you where she went."

The soldier said, "Put your hands down. Relax." He turned and called back to the jeep, "They're clear. This is Duane Connors." He turned back to Cindy and asked in a non-threatening tone, "Are you Lance Corporal Sing?"

Before Cindy could answer, two Black Hawk helicopters erupted over the treetops from the south, flared severely, and settled into a low hover twenty yards down the highway. The pilot of the lead helicopter (Black Hawk One) soft-landed, facing Duane and Cindy. Duane could see the pilot's tactical helmet through the helicopter's wind-screen.

Cindy took a couple of steps toward Duane and shouted, "No, my name is Cindy Mathews. I'm Duane's girlfriend."

The soldier looked back at Duane and asked with a touch of irritation in is voice, "Why is she here?" Duane took note of the insignia of an Army Sergeant on the soldier's sleeve.

"My truck broke down, Sergeant. Cindy gave me a ride."

The sergeant thought about this for a moment, then nodded.

"Where is Lance Corporal Sing?"

Duane pointed at the mouth of the dirt driveway. He shouted over the sound of the beating rotors, "When I left here at 12:30, she ran back up that dirt driveway. She said that she was going to prevent the men from leaving. She said that there was a small hunting cabin, a pole barn, and large gravel parking lot about a mile up the road. She also said that she was the only female on site. She asked that you be careful and not shoot her."

In one motion, the soldier nodded, stepped away from Duane, pointed at the driveway, keyed his radio, and said, "Dirt road at your two o'clock, one to one point five clicks, cabin, pole barn, gravel parking lot. Lance Corporal Sing is believed to be only female on site, Sir."

The pilot of the Black Hawk One responded with a curt, "Roger that."

Black Hawk One rose like a shot, tilted forward, and disappeared over the desert. As soon as Black Hawk One's tail rotor passed over the edge of the desert alongside the driveway, Black Hawk Two followed suit. In an instant, they were gone, and silence filled the scene.

The soldier turned back to Duane, "Sir, do you have some form of ID?"

As Duane was digging his wallet out of his back pocket, the soldier asked the same question of Cindy.

"I have my driver's license," Cindy answered, "It's in my purse. I'll get it." Cindy started to take a step toward her car.

"No," the soldier said and put up his hand. The soldier called over Cindy's shoulder, "Please, get Miss Mathew's purse from the vehicle."

The sergeant said, "I apologize for the rough reception. All stateside Army commands have ordered that all agencies address initial contact situations as though they are terrorist positive. The National Security

Agency has been tracking electronic chatter that indicated the possibility of such attacks. We weren't sure if you kidnapped Corporal Sing and used her as bait for an ambush."

Duane answered, "That's all right. I'd rather you take extra precautions and verify my identity than get caught off guard and get us both hurt." As they talked, the sergeant led Duane and Cindy to his jeep.

"Please, hold your driver's license up beside your face."

The sergeant took Duane's picture with a small camera and then repeated the process with Cindy. He put the camera away and took out a palm-sized video camera. He turned the camera on himself and said without embellishment, "Sergeant Robert Davis, Military Police Detachment Investigation Division, Fourth Army Command, Fort Sill, Oklahoma, 0305 hours, June 16, 2015. I am standing on Highway 49 thirty miles north and west of Fort Sill, Oklahoma. I am taking the first statement of Duane Connors, Medicine Creek, Oklahoma: witness in the matter of two stolen nuclear weapons and the disappearance of Lance Corporal Cassandra Sing, USMC, this night from Fort Sill, Oklahoma."

Sergeant Davis lowered the camera a moment and addressed Duane, "First statements are most accurate when taken as soon after an incident as possible. Do you mind?"

Duane shook his head.

Sergeant Davis raised the camera to Duane. "Mr. Connors, you may consult an attorney before you make a statement if you'd be more comfortable. I will advise you that you aren't a suspect of any crime at this time. If you're willing to make a statement look into the camera, state your name and place of birth, then, tell me what happened tonight. Start at the beginning and try not to leave anything out."

Duane looked at the camera, "My name is Duane Connors …"

Chapter Nineteen

Brian's pilot called ahead and obtained permission to land at the Fort Sill Military Police Tactical Heliport. Before Brian could step down from the S-300, the pilot tapped the earpiece on his headset. Brian readjusted his own headset and keyed his monitor button.

The pilot indicated his gauges and said, "I have to go refuel. I'll be back in fifteen."

Brian gave him a thumbs-up and stepped away from the Sikorsky. An Army Corporal met him and said, "Mr. Sing, follow me, Sir."

The non-commissioned officer (NCO) led Brian to the MP-OIC in the crisis control center.

Brian asked, "Any word about my niece?"

By way of an answer, the MP-OIC handed Brian a copy of the transcript from Duane's phone call. "We received a phone call fifteen minutes ago." The MP-OIC waited for Brian to read the message.

"Sounds like Lance Corporal Sing is trying to take down an armed domestic terrorist cell all by herself."

Brian nodded and thought *that would be Cassie.*

"She sounds like a real badass, Sir. We've dispatched a ground unit and two Black Hawks with a hostage rescue team on board to the site indicated in the phone call. If you'll have a seat, I'll keep you informed as the situation develops. Corporal, get Mr. Sing a fresh cup of coffee."

Brian ignored the request to sit down and instead said, "I'm going to the site. There may be two nuclear weapons on the ground there. My niece is there. How did the thieves get a hold of two nuclear weapons?" Brian designed the last question to sidetrack any objections to Brian going to the field site.

"We are investigating that question as we speak, Sir." However, I can't authorize you to enter what we believe is an active shooter situation. We have two dead MPs."

Without hesitation, Brian answered, "The President of the United States authorized me to enter the situation."

After a pause to formulate his answer, the MP-OIC asked, "Are you armed, Sir?"

Brian shook his head.

The MP-OIC went to a gun safe and returned with a holstered forty-five. He said, "I'd feel more secure with the decision if you were armed, Sir. The location we were given is on a state highway, twenty-eight miles northwest of Fort Sill. We will set up a forward tactical center on the highway one mile east of where we believe the cabin is located. If you'll agree to wait at the forward tactical center until the site is secure, I'll have the GPS coordinates radioed to your pilot."

Brian took the weapon out of the holster and put it in the side pocket of his dinner jacket. It was a meaningless concession. Brian never saw the need to be armed.

"I agree to wait if you'll remind the tactical unit that there's an unarmed female U.S. Marine, possibly no longer in uniform, on the site."

"I'll remind them, Sir."

Brian headed for the roof.

The MP-OIC called aloud, "Everybody, eyes up here. I'm reducing our security status to yellow. Maintain the extra guards on the gates and the perimeter. Maintain the lockdown of the weapons maintenance facility. The north gate is an active crime scene and closed to all traffic until further notice. All other base facilities and services may return to normal operations. Open the base, ladies and gentlemen."

*****

When Brian emerged onto the roof a minute later, the Sikorsky was gone. He was about to go back downstairs when he noticed a small, bright light approaching his location, quite low to the ground and moving like a rocket. Ten seconds later, the Sikorsky sat down uncomfortably close and unbelievably fast next to Brian. Brian boarded the helicopter and put on his headset.

"Sorry for the delay, Sir. The Army wouldn't take my state police credit card, so I charged the fuel to you. I received a set of GPS coordinates a few minutes ago. I take it we're going to that location?"

Before Brian could answer, the pilot entered the coordinates into his navigation system. Brian keyed his talk toggle and answered, anyway.

"We are. There's a tactical hostage rescue team headed there, also. Can you find out what com frequency they're using, and can we listen to their transmissions?"

"See what I can do, Sir."

The Sikorsky lifted off like a carnival ride, and the pilot headed northwest.

Chapter Twenty

Just before 3:10 a.m., Brian's Sikorsky swooped down to a fast and frightening, but otherwise perfect landing at the forward tactical center on Highway 49.

"Air Cav.?" Brian asked.

"Yes, Sir, Army Air Cavalry. Two tours in Afghanistan," the pilot said with a deadpan smile.

An older civilian car and an Army jeep were parked in the middle of the road fifty feet from the Sikorsky. A knot of men stood next to the jeep and talked animatedly. Brian saw more soldiers and barricades blocking the road one hundred yards up and one hundred yards down the road. Brian thought that the barricades were more of a procedural curtesy because there wasn't much road traffic in the Oklahoma outback at 4:30 in the morning. The milk truck that Cassie mentioned wasn't going to get away.

Brian walked over to the highest-ranking soldier. Above the roar of the helicopter, he said, "My name is Brian Sing. What's the situation? Have you found Corporal Sing, yet?"

The soldier brought Brian up to speed then pointed to Duane. Brian nodded and clapped the man on the shoulder. Brian stepped up to Duane and waited for the officer who was questioning Duane to acknowledge him.

When the officer finished writing in his casebook and looked at Brian, Brian introduced himself, "Lieutenant, my name is Brian Sing."

"Lieutenant St. John, Sir. We've been expecting you, Sir. This is Duane Connors. He is the one who last spoke to Lance Corporal Sing and the one who relayed the call to the MP desk."

Brian looked at Duane, extended his hand. "Brian Sing. You talked to Cassie earlier?"

"It's a pleasure, Sir. Yes, Sir. Or rather, she talked to me. She's a real firebrand, Sir." Duane meant it as a compliment.

"Do you know where she is?"

"Yes, Sir. She told me that she was returning to the cabin to keep an eye on the situation."

Brian turned to the officer. "I'm going to wait in my bird and monitor communications. As soon as the site is secure, I'm going in."

The officer waved an agreement and said, "They are Army tactical 107.6, Sir."

"Thank you."

Brian returned to the Sikorsky, put on his headset, and waited.

Chapter Twenty-One

In an instant, the scene in front of Cassie changed in her favor. Four of the men were in the cabin and seemed to be staying there. A tall, blond man stood by the rollup door. The sixth man came out of the barn. It was Flat Top. He crossed the open space between the barn and the cabin like a man on a mission. He bypassed the front door and went around to the back.

He's checking the generator, she thought.

She looked back at the blond man by the barn door. He started walking toward her, then paused twenty feet from where Cassie hid. He turned to face one of the debris piles, laid his weapon on the butt end of a wood stump, took two steps toward the next debris pile, and stopped. He angled his face toward the sky a bit and bent over a bit at the waist.

Cassie realized that the blond man was preparing to urinate. The lights around the parking lot went out. The milk truck still illuminated a patch of desert beyond the barn, but Cassie and Blondie were plunged into near total darkness. Her eyes were slow to adjust to the abrupt change, but the advantage was hers. Though still blinded by the darkness, Cassie sprang to her feet and started running toward Blondie. She knew from experience that by the time she reached him, her vision would improve enough for her to see him.

Cassie's legs were stiff from the miles of running earlier and the following hours of sitting. Her knees and ankles wouldn't flex properly. Still, she sprinted as fast as she could. Three steps from Blondie, Cassie planted her left foot on the side of an abandoned commercial truck tire and launched herself into the air. Her feet came up in front of her so that she was flying prone in the air. Once off the ground, she threw her left arm across her chest and her right arm behind her back. This rotated Cassie's body in the air so that she was airborne on her left side, shoulder height to Blondie. She pulled her knees up to her chest and her feet as close to her hips as she could. When her feet were eighteen inches from Blondie's shoulders, she kicked out with all the explosiveness she had in her.

*****

As far as Blondie knew, the plan was for him to drive the milk truck when the crew left their hideout. Milk trucks were a common pre-dawn fleet in Oklahoma. Dairymen

195

milked their cows late in the evening and again before dawn. The first round of product pickup for the day started a 3:00 a.m. Blondie believed that when he left the hideout, he would blend in with the rest of the milk truck fleet from the various dairy distributers and drive unnoticed to the warehouse in Oklahoma City.

There would be no time for a break before the crew reached the Oklahoma City warehouse. If he wanted to relieve himself, it would have to be now. He walked to the debris field, put his pistol down, and took two steps.

He closed his eyes and tilted his face up to the night sky as he let the relief flow. He never knew what hit him. One instant, he was urinating, and the next, he was falling forward with no feeling in his body.

Cassie had kicked Blondie in the middle of his spine at the top of his shoulder blades. Blondie's body absorbed all the momentum from Cassie's body and snapped forward with an amazing amount of force. Unfortunately, Blondie's head didn't make the same transition. The joint between the second and third cervical vertebrae took the brunt of the trauma and his head snapped back, ripping the joint open. The force of the

movement damaged the soft connective tissues at the front of the spine. The loss of in-
tegrity of the soft tissues allowed the joint to
separate even further.

When Blondie's head had reached
full backward extension, it rebounded forward as though on a spring. When his head
reached full flexion, the strain and sudden
change of direction did the same damage to
the back of the spine between the second and
third vertebrae. Blondie had the most extreme case of whiplash imaginable. Had all
motion stopped at that time, he might have
someday recovered, but Cassie's kick was
too forceful. His head bounced off his chest
and rolled back with a violent snap. This
time, the soft tissues in the middle of the
spine separated. When Blondie hit the
ground, he was paralyzed but still conscious.

Blondie's heart didn't stop when his
body lost communication with his brain. The
beats were erratic and lower pressure, but
they were enough. He stayed conscious and
lay face down in the dirt. He knew that he
wasn't breathing but couldn't draw a breath.
His lungs wouldn't inflate. Someone flipped
him over on his back as his panic rose. Out
of the corner of his eye, he could see a girl
beside him. Every instinct made him want to

cry out for help, but nothing would come out. In a few seconds, Blondie couldn't distinguish between the dark sky overhead and his darkening vision.

*****

After the kick, it seemed to Cassie that she hung in the air forever. After what seemed an eternity, she fell and landed hard on her left side in the dirt. She recoiled to an upright position on the first bounce. She picked up the pistol and ejected the clip from the butt of the gun. She looked at the top of the clip, saw bullets, and assumed that the clip was full. She reinserted the clip and chambered a round. Then, she turned her attention to Blondie. She turned him over and searched his pockets.

Damn, no cell phone and no extra clips. These guys are worse than morons. How are they supposed to defend themselves when they don't carry any extra ammunition?

Cassie found a set of mixed keys, which she pocketed. She might need a way out of here later. Her situation had improved; she was armed and there were only five more armed assailants left to deal with. She had a new plan. She could run the length of the barn before anyone came out of the cabin and before Flat Top came out from behind the cabin. She would turn the corner and unload a few rounds into each of the milk truck's front tires and into the radiator and engine for good measure. After disabling the milk truck, she would just keep running into the desert. She knew she could evade the men until help arrived. Cassie would have one dead bad guy, the license plate numbers for all the vehicles, and the milk truck disabled. All she needed to do was stay alive. She turned to run the length of the barn in the dark.

*****

Flat Top walked across the parking area and around to the back of the cabin. The cadre would be leaving in a few minutes. It was time to turn everything off, shut down the generator, and clean up a few details. The lights going out was the signal for the four to maneuver the two expendable members into the cabin. When all six men were in the cabin, the staff reductions would commence. Flat Top turned off the generator, and the men in the cabin turned on two small electric camp lanterns to compensate for the loss of the permanent lights. Flat Top was sure that they would catch the dead-men-walking off guard. Everything was coming together nicely.

Flat Top left the generator and walked around the edge of the cabin. He intended to call Blondie into the cabin but saw what he thought was Blondie kneeling between two of the debris piles and wondered what the goof was doing now. He had only taken two steps when he realized that the person kneeling in the debris piles wasn't a member of their crew. Then he saw the feet sticking out. He took two more steps and recognized the tan digital Marine work pants and tan combat boots. They had an intruder, and the intruder was military. Flat Top's first impulse was to shout for the intruder to stop. He stifled that impulse and decided to get closer before making his presence known. Flat Top was, by nature, mean and used his sadistic streak to make some of his more brutal activities more entertaining.

Flat Top raised his gun to fire a couple of shots at the intruder to get his attention. He didn't want to kill the intruder just yet. He wanted to play with him. Flat Top wanted to watch the intruder's eyes as he inflicted pain on him for the fun of it. He could always kill him later. For Flat Top, the game was on. But, before he could bring his gun all the way up, the intruder started running along the face of the darken barn. Flat Top was stunned when he realized that the intruder was a girl and that she was carrying a gun in her right hand.

Flat Top had never faced an armed opponent before. Facing off with an opponent who could defend herself would be a new experience. He reveled in the added element of danger. He might face the remote possibility of injury during the frivolities. Flat Top had always enjoyed hurting living things--animals when he was a child and people as he grew older. Lately, he considered bar fights a form of recreation. The part he liked the most was continuing to kick and beat an opponent after his victim had quit defending himself. Flat Top also enjoyed a more secretive pastime. He relished snatching, torturing, raping, and then killing young women. Seeing the fear in their faces and hearing panic in their voices made him feel powerful, like a god. The rush reinforced his conviction that his strength and willingness to use his power put him in control of his world. It entitled him. And since he had never been caught or punished for his brutality, he felt vindicated, invincible. He would always get away with it. To Flat Top, his willingness to release his sadistic tendencies gave him identity.

But this was something new. This girl has the ability to fight back. She could make me work for my pleasure. She could hurt or even kill me. These thoughts crossed Flat Top's mind as he took a couple of steps. He reveled in the possibility. He would hurt her, and he would kill her. She would be powerless to stop him. He was a superior, entitled, privileged human being. He walked toward the barn like he envisioned himself an old west gunslinger. He raised his gun.

*****

Cassie had taken five or six steps when the metal siding on the barn in front of her erupted in a flurry of frenetic fireworks. Her adrenaline spiked. She heard the soft *tink, tink* of bullets hitting the barn. Someone was shooting at her! She could tell from where the bullets hit that the shooter had tried to lead her as a bird hunter would a flying pheasant. However, like every other trait these men displayed, he was an amateur. He had led her too much, and he had missed.

Cassie planted her left foot and spun around to head away from the barrage of bullets that blocked her path. As she spun, she sprayed a short burst into the darkness at the side of the cabin. She knew that there was little chance for her to hit anybody during the maneuver, but she hoped it would convince the shooter to pause and duck.

She had lost one advantage; they knew she was here. She could still make this plan work if she could get around the corner of the barn. She could run down the length of the barn, fire a couple of random shots at the milk truck tires as she ran past the open door, and still withdraw to the desert.

Cassie had only taken two steps when another volley of bullets hit the barn in front of her. She thought, *He can't have made the same mistake twice. He's toying with me; big mistake.*

Cassie planted her right foot to change direction this time and spun to her left. She could see the silhouette of a man walking across the parking lot toward her. She pulled the trigger to spray a line of shots in his direction but was shocked when there was one shot and then a click. Her gun was empty.

Six bullets in the gun, that's all? Why even carry a gun? These people are idiots.

After the misfire, Cassie planted her right foot to change direction yet again. She hoped the ruse of two quick turns would cause her attacker to shoot behind her and allow her time to make it to the end of the barn. Then, she would run off into the desert. Her gun was empty, and she had no replacement clips. She was unarmed. More importantly, she had lost her best chance to disable the milk truck.

*****

Flat Top wasn't in a hurry. He wanted to extend this part of his game. He had fired a burst in front of the girl to turn her around on purpose. He also intended for the second round of shots to be in front of the girl, not to hit her. He wanted to turn her around again. This was rather like shooting at a tin duck at a carnival shooting game. He couldn't hear anything except the pounding of his pulse inside his eardrums. The rush of blood was palpable. He could taste it. He could feel the tingle on his skin. His eyes were wide and glassy. He didn't allow himself to see anything except the girl. He didn't care how long it had been since he last blinked. He didn't want to miss a single moment of his kill.

Flat Top miscalculated his aim on the second round of shots that he fired at the girl. He continued the volley too long. The girl spun twice and stepped into his line of fire. Flat Top knew that she was alone. No one shot at him when he shot at her. She was his. He continued to walk toward her.

*****

Either Cassie completed her second turn sooner than she expected, or the shooter continued his volley longer than she expected. It made no difference which. Cassie was facing the corner of the barn and almost ran into the shower of sparks from the second barrage of shots. She tried to stem her forward momentum, but it was too late. Yielding to instinct, she threw her forearms up in front of her face to intercept the sparks. She still wanted to make the corner of the barn if the shots stopped. The shooter's clip must be empty by now. The wait lasted the length of a breath, but it seemed like an eternity.

The blow felt like a hammer hitting her in the left elbow. The bullet tore through the back of her left arm above the elbow but below the triceps muscle. Before Cassie could react, her arm went numb. The impact and Cassie's remaining momentum spun Cassie a quarter turn to her right. She was facing the barn when the second shot hit.

The second bullet hit her in the back, two inches above the left hipbone and two inches from the left side. The impact threw her forward a half step and up against the barn. Unable to fend off the collision with the barn with her injured left arm, Cassie bounced off the siding and fell onto the gravel driveway. Unlike the first wound, the shot to her torso hurt like hell. The bullet burned all the way through. The pain inside her abdomen was like someone pinching a tab of tender skin and then twisting.

Cassie was on her back on the ground. She was nauseated. The pain came in spasms. It felt like someone had shoved a metal tennis ball into her belly and up against her diaphragm. She coughed with pain when she breathed out. The tennis ball kept her from breathing in. The still night air got colder.

Cassie pushed with all the strength she had to turn until she could see the man walking toward her across the gravel parking lot. The effort left her wanting to throw up. She didn't realize how fast she was breathing. Cassie stole a glance at the cabin. No one had come out. She was still one-on-one with Flat Top. The situation wasn't as bad as it could have been. She lifted the gun to Flat Top. If she could have mustered the focus, she would have thrown it at him.

Cassie watched Flat Top approach. She could see him grinning with excitement. His wide eyes held a depth of crazy. His was a game that only the insane can understand.

She knew that a herd of buffalo could have stampeded between them, and Flat Top wouldn't have noticed. He walked to within a few feet of her and stopped. She could hear him breathing.

Come a little closer, she thought. *Just a little closer.*

Without saying anything or changing his facial expression, he raised the pistol.

Snap-ching, snap-ching, snap-ching, snap-ching. Cassie heard the four shots and her consciousness screamed. Her mind reeled and retreated a step or two from reality. She slammed her eyes shut and clenched them hard. She didn't want to face what came next. Her body stiffened despite the pain in her side. Every muscle in her body tightened as if a tight muscle could stem the flow of blood from a bullet hole. She held her breath and waited for either the pain or the numbness to assault her. In the years to come, Cassie would never discuss the emotions, thoughts, prayers, and words that she experienced in those horrible moments. She faced the moment of her death. By the grace of God, the moment passed, and she kept her reactions to that instant a secret.

Chapter Twenty-Two

From the pilot's seat of his Black Hawk, Captain Jamison, U. S. Army Aviation, turned to look where the civilian was pointing. He could see the dirt driveway and acknowledged the verbal confirmation. Black Hawk One lifted off the pavement without hesitation. He understood that the cabin was a click or two inland from his position and he wanted to be there–now. He nosed over to gain speed as soon as his skids cleared the tops of the roadside brush. He had a team of six field-equipped soldiers and one experienced field medic in the back of his ride. He was determined to make sure that when he arrived at the cabin, everyone present would understand that he was in charge.

Black Hawk Two followed Jamison's lead. It also had a six-man combat strike team and a medic. Whatever Jamison did in Black Hawk One, Black Hawk Two would assume a left-side flanking position and cover Jamison. The two pilots had flown into dozens of similar hot zones in three different countries over the years. They could predict each other's moves. Twenty seconds in, Jamison could see the glow of lights ahead and turned to intercept. He had just fixed his vision on the spot when the lights went out. He was concerned that someone had heard the choppers coming. The hot zone may have just gotten hotter. He didn't ease up on the collective. He dropped his night vision goggles into place and turned them on.

He keyed his com unit and announced, "Eyes up. The bogies might know we're inbound. Go infrared."

He saw the barn first, then the cabin. The milk truck headlights overstimulated his night vision goggles, so he turned the gain down as the gravel parking lot came into view. The scene was just as his intel had described. He couldn't see fine detail in the darker areas, but he knew what was happening on the ground by the back of the barn. He yawed the Black Hawk a quarter turn to the left so that he was still flying to the gravel parking lot. He was just flying sideways.

He keyed his mic, "Sergeant Makleroy, left side of the barn, on the ground, female Marine down, male shooter standing. Take him out."

Sergeant Makleroy, a veteran of two tours in Iraq, hefted his weapon from between his knees and slapped his flying harness's quick release. In one motion, he pulled the side door's release lever, slid open the door, and dropped to a sitting position on the lower doorframe with his left foot on the skid and his right foot dangling. As he settled, he turned on his night vision and chambered a round. The bogie was lifting his weapon. Makleroy didn't have time to relax, take a calming breath, or aim. He didn't want to take a chance at hitting the Marine on the ground, so he fired a four-shot burst designed to unzip the bogie from the bottom to the top, not side-to-side.

The burst was right on target and did its job. The first shot hit the bogie across the front of the thighs, eliminating his ability to stand. The second shot tore through his abdomen, eviscerating the man. Flat Top lost blood pressure and consciousness because of the second shot. The third shot entered the bogie just below the upraised arm and shattered some ribs as it entered the chest cavity. The bullet turned his lungs and heart to mush and broke more ribs exiting the body. The fourth bullet grazed the bogie's back half an inch above the shoulder blades, blasting the spine. Unlike Blondie, Flat Top was dead before he started to fall.

*****

Four loud gunshots! Cassie's subconsciousness screamed.

An instant after the shots, with her mind still screaming, Cassie searched her body with her one good hand for the warm, sticky feel of blood. Her hand raced to every sensation and itch, expecting the worst. She felt for body damage and torn clothing. There was nothing out of the ordinary. She breathed slower and then slower still.

Four loud rifle shots, Cassie. Her mind raged.

Slack-faced, Cassie opened her eyes. She muttered to herself, "Those were M-16 rifle shots."

Relief poured over her like cold water. She examined her body and couldn't find any new bullet wounds. There was no ripped clothing, no gaping wounds. She eased her gaze around to where Flat Top had been standing. All she could see was the cloud of dust settling on his boots and lower legs. The pain in her side returned. Once again, she couldn't breathe, and nausea flooded back.

Four rifle shots, Cassie. The cavalry has arrived. Cassie looked above her shoulder. Through blurred vision, she could see the Black Hawk scabbing in from the west. Cassie watched two soldiers jump from the Black Hawk and run toward her. She let the empty pistol slip out of her right hand and pointed to the cabin.

Chapter Twenty-Three

Captain Jamison flared Black Hawk One sideways into a hover eighteen inches above the ground with his right flank still exposed to the gravel driveway. Black Hawk Two flanked around Black Hawk One on the left and flared into a similar hover above a small, grass-covered hill. His job was to cover Jamison's left side and the back of the cabin.

Before Black Hawk One became stable in the air, Sergeant Makleroy stepped off the skid and took off in a crouching run toward the downed Marine. He kept his weapon raised and in the firing position as he ran. He assumed that the Marine was wounded since she didn't get up after Flat Top went down. A wounded Marine was exposed and defenseless in a proven killing field, and that was unacceptable to Makleroy.

Before Sergeant Makleroy could take his second step, Army Medic Corporal Jeremy Hong stepped off the Black Hawk behind him. Corporal Hong also assumed that the downed Marine was wounded. Seconds might make a difference. This was what Hong was trained for.

Makleroy knew that there must be more armed bogies somewhere in the arena. He knew that they might be watching and could open fire at any moment. He hoped that the presence of the other soldiers and the Black Hawks had convinced the bad guys to keep their heads down, but he knew that they could cut him down at any second.

Makleroy never wavered. *Courage isn't the lack of fear. Courage is the presence of action despite fear.* Makleroy's mouth was dry. He could feel them watching him. He felt exposed but not alone. Makleroy was the picture of determination. His eyes never quit searching the scene before him as he rushed to secure that wounded Marine.

*****

Hong ran one step behind Makleroy with the same dedication and courage. The difference was that Hong was unarmed. He knew that he could die in an instant, as well. Corporal Hong hoped that the red cross emblazoned across his chest and hat would deter any aggression aimed his way. Hong's weapon of choice was the array of small medical kits, supplies, and devices that he carried. He ran across the killing field with as much courage as Makleroy. There was a wounded Marine out there and he was going to help her.

Makleroy was halfway across the open expanse of gravel when he saw Cassie point at the cabin. Makleroy took the gesture to mean that the bogies were in the cabin. He shifted aim from the grounds around Cassie to the front of the cabin and felt the dozen men behind him follow his lead. None of the men took any action that might result in open gunfire as long as Cassie was in the open.

*****

Even though the cabin was quiet, neither The Major nor the three other men heard the rotor sounds of the Black Hawks. The men waited for Flat Top and Blondie to return to the cabin so that The Major could give them a pep talk before they started their caravan to Oklahoma City.

The report of four M-16 shots alerted them that the Army had arrived. The Major ordered the others to turn off the electric lanterns. He stepped over to one of the windows and peeked through a slit beside the blanket covering the window without touching the cloth. He could see the thinnest slice of the gravel driveway in front of the cabin. He didn't like what he saw. Two soldiers were running across the open gravel expanse. If there were two soldiers, there were a dozen soldiers. One of the running soldiers was carrying an M-16 pointed at his window. He recoiled as if he knew the soldier was about to shoot. He shifted his gaze and saw the tips of the spinning rotor and a portion of the tail section of the Black Hawk hovering over the gravel.

The Army was here. His plans just got more complicated. He wasn't going to be able to drive away scot free with his nukes. He had to think. Selling the nukes would net him a lot of money. A lot of money meant a nice retirement for him in someplace tropical, like Belize or Brazil. He didn't intend to let the Army screw up his retirement.

The Major was delusional enough to think that if he created the correct diversion, he could drive the milk truck out of the compound without the Army noticing. He was convinced that he was smarter than the Army outside. Surely, they'd be stupid enough to let the milk truck pass. *After all, it's just a milk truck.*

The Major still faced the window. He said over his shoulder, "The war for the Constitution has started. Move up to the windows. We'll hold them off from here."

The three men stayed where they were. Flea, in a moment of clear thinking, said, "That's the Army out there. I'm not going to fight the Army. They'll kill us."

The Major turned and shot Flea. Flea dropped to the floor. As Flea liked to say, 'he dropped like a sack of stupid.'

The Major growled an order to the other two, "Move up to the windows. We can still save this day for the revolution."

He turned back to the window. The man standing behind The Major raised his gun and shot The Major. Now, there were two sacks of stupid lying on the floor. The two remaining men looked at each other across a ten-foot chasm. Both still had their weapons in their hands. Neither knew that both weapons were now empty. One gun didn't have any bullets in it to begin with. The other shooter had just used the last of his. They were like the saying, "bringing a knife to gun fight" except these two losers brought two empty guns to a gun fight. Both seemed to be weighing their chances of surviving the potential shootout.

One of them asked, "What do we do, now?"

"I don't know about you, but I'm going to do whatever the Army tells me to do. I do know two things: I'm not going to die for this so-called revolution, and I'm not going anywhere near those windows."

Both men looked at the windows and took a small step away from them. When they looked back at each other, they dropped their weapons on the floor at the same time. Like true revolutionaries, they cowered in fear.

*****

Makleroy slid to a stop on one knee alongside Cassie in a direct line between her and the cabin. He kept his rifle up, his finger on the trigger, and his aiming eye scanning the front of the cabin. Makleroy was the picture of calm, but he dared anyone in the cabin to flick an ear or cough sideways.

Hong slid to a stop on both knees at Cassie's side. He knew that he could rely on Makleroy's protective shield to cover him as well as his patient. He dropped his kits and supplies and started his triage. There were no head wounds or chest wounds. He saw no evidence of an explosion or traumatic impact. There were two wounds: one to the left arm and one to the left side. The patient was having trouble breathing.

As Hong worked, Makleroy barked, "Marine, sitrep!"

Cassie's thoughts were swimming. She was having trouble focusing. She felt like she couldn't breathe. The command elicited a moment of clarity. Her response reflected her training. Cassie pointed at the cabin and, between labored breaths, said, "Four or five bogies in the cabin, armed with automatic, silenced pistols. They killed MPs at Fort Sill. I believe the barn is unoccupied. Two nuclear weapons in secret compartment back of the milk truck." In a rush, she added, "The deuce and a half is a suicide bomb. Don't approach." Cassie couldn't think of anything else to say.

As Cassie made her report, Makleroy repeated every word into his com unit. When he reported Cassie's belief that the barn was deserted, the two men on the far right of the offensive arc detached from the line and ran to either side of the barn's rollup door. With quick steps down the length of the barn and back, they searched it. When they returned, they both took up defensive positions at the door. One keyed his com and reported, "Barn is clear."

As Cassie spoke, Hong cut her shirt up the left side exposing her gunshot wound. For now, he ignored the wound in the arm. It wasn't life threatening, and the bleeding had slowed. Hong rinsed the site of the wound with a saline solution to remove the blood, sand, and gravel so he could assess the wound. There was a small hole in the back with a larger hole in the front. The gunshot was a through-and-through. The wound was also not life threatening.

Hong poured a powerful disinfectant and antibiotic on the wound and slapped a self-adhesive field dressing over the area. He asked Cassie, "Marine, you have trouble breathing. Is it a throat obstruction or chest problem?"

"Pressure in chest from below. It's painful to take a breath."

Hong opened his field drug kit and took out a pre-loaded, half-grain Morphine Syrette and jabbed it into Cassie's hip. After the injection, Hong broke the thin plastic cover off the grease pencil mounted on the back of the field syringe. He wrote the date, time, type of drug, and the dosage on Cassie's abdomen above the field dressing. He didn't want anyone to dose her again too soon.

"That should help. Gun shot in the hip, gun shot in the left elbow, are you wounded anywhere else?"

Cassie shook her head. Hong took a field splint out of his backpack and depressed the hinge release. The splint pivoted open like a compass used to draw circles. When the angle of the splint was close to the angle of Cassie's injured elbow, Hong released the catch. He slid the splint under Cassie's arm and wrapped the arm and splint with an Ace bandage to stabilize them. He didn't find evidence of broken bones, but he didn't want to risk exacerbating any nerve damage.

Cassie wanted to say, "Ooh, that took the pain away."

What came out was, "Ooooo."

Cassie's eyes rolled back in her head, and the pain drained from her face.

Makleroy finished his report and released his com button. He said, "We need to move, Hong." To Cassie he said, "We have located the deuce and a half and are working to neutralize it now. Good work, Marine."

Cassie didn't seem to hear him. Makleroy glared at Hong and raised his eyebrows.

Hong said, "She's stable enough to move. None of her wounds are life threatening. I'm ready when you are." Then he added, "Mack, they shot her in the back."

Makleroy keyed his com unit, "Captain Jamison, patient is stable and ready to move at your command." Makleroy's pause was pregnant with tension. His next words were electric, "Sir, they shot her in the back."

Jamison heard the report. He could feel the bile of his anger rising. Jamison's co-pilot heard the report. The pilot and co-pilot of Black Hawk Two heard the report. The soldiers standing at the protective perimeter heard the report. Everyone monitoring the tactical frequency heard the report.

Jamison elevated Black Hawk One to ten feet off the ground, and Black Hawk Two followed suit. Then, Jamison keyed his com unit, "Okay, gentlemen, eyes up! We're moving the patient. Go, Makleroy!"

Makleroy reached down with his left hand and looped his fingers under Cassie's right armpit. He didn't look away from the cabin. He didn't lower his weapon. Hong put a couple of pieces of equipment on Cassie's torso, grabbed her canvas belt with one hand, and cradled her head with the other.

With Hong guiding them, the two men lifted Cassie and moved her ten steps into the debris field. Cassie was out of the kill zone.

Hong put a blood pressure cuff on Cassie's right arm and a pulse rate monitor on one of her fingers. Makleroy keyed his com unit, "Patient is secure, Sir."

Jamison keyed his com unit and said in an angry monotone, "Understood." Then hc raised his voice to command level and added, "Okay, boys, light 'em up." He reached up to his overhead console and turned on his twin seal-beamed search and rescue spotlights and trained them on the front of the cabin. Black Hawk Two illuminated the side of the cabin and the area behind the cabin. A dozen soldiers turned on their red targeting lasers. The area lit up like a rock concert.

Jamison keyed his public address system and ordered, "In the cabin. Open the front door. Throw out your weapons. Come out one at a time with your hands up and your palms open. You have thirty seconds."

Then, for emphasis, Jamison did something that was out of character, contrary to standing orders, and against the law in the Continental United States. He triggered the twin twenty-millimeter cannons mounted on the underside of the Black Hawk and unleashed a burst of six rounds along the length of the highest roofline of the cabin. Against the law or not, Jamison got tremendous satisfaction from the display of his authority.

Each cannon round made a six-inch hole in the front of the roof and an eighteen-inch hole coming out the other side. The cannon shells reduced the impacted roofing materials to confetti. Forty years of accumulated dust and sand erupted into a dry fog and mixed with the pulverized roofing materials. The impact blew some of the mix into the desert and the rest floated down into the great room of the cabin like a fine snow. The dust, dirt, and roofing debris caught and reflected the red targeting lasers.

One of the men repeatedly yelled, "I give up."

The other man just sounded like a screaming siren at full volume.

Fifteen seconds passed before the two men followed orders. The door to the cabin opened, and the two men inside threw out a handful of rifles and pistols that landed like broom handles out of a utility closet. They walked out of the cabin door, one behind the other, with their arms up and their hands splayed.

Jamison expected four to six men to surrender. When only two men came out, he keyed his PA system and demanded, "Where are the others?"

From inside the hovering helicopter, Jamison couldn't hear the man's answer. One of the GIs closest to the surrendering men reported, "He said the others are dead, Sir."

Jamison ordered, "Eyes up on the back of the structure. Front rank, take the structure, two on two."

Two soldiers moved toward the front of the cabin. After they had run a couple of steps, two more stood up. In four seconds, eight soldiers from various places around the defensive semicircle were on the move.

The first two GIs pushed both surrendering men backward violently. As the men tried to compensate by stepping back, the GIs violently pulled both forward. Both suspects landed face down in the gravel. The GIs shouted orders as fast as they could.

"Get down! Move! Feet up! Arms out front! Palms open and up! Move! I will shoot to kill!"

It wasn't until one of the GIs placed a size fourteen combat boot across the back of his neck and ground his face into the gravel, that the first surrendering man wet himself. The other man continued to scream.

The next four GIs rushed the open cabin door. The first two took up covering positions outside the door and the next two sprinted through the open door and searched for targets.

The first GI inside the cabin screamed, "Doors, Doors," and aimed his sighting laser at the closed doors on the end of the cabin. Two more GIs entered the cabin and yanked them open. One was an empty closet, and the other was a cesspool of a bathroom.

All the GIs in the cabin shouted "clear" at once. While two watched the interior of the cabin, the rest turned their focus to the cabin's back door.

"Structure clear. Ready to exit at back door."

Jamison answered, "Understood, cabin is clear. Heads up, everybody. Friendlies coming out of back door of structure." Jamison didn't want any surprises.

Two GIs exited the back and scanned the open fields beyond. One reported, "Back perimeter secure. Area of operation is clear."

"Perimeter is secure. Move to a defensive perimeter."

As one, the soldiers moved closer to the cabin, turned, and trained their weapons on the surrounding desert. Captain Jamison was now in charge of this theater of operation.

Jamison let his Black Hawk settle on the gravel driveway, keyed his com unit, and ordered, "Hong, move the patient to Black Hawk Two for medevac. Black Hawk Two, you're now life-flight to Fort Sill."

Hong continued to assess Cassie's condition. Her breathing seemed less strained, her color was returning, and she wasn't bleeding excessively. She was stable enough for evacuation. Black Hawk Two's medic arrived next to Cassie with a field litter. The two medics loaded her onto the litter while Makleroy watched. Makleroy slung his weapon onto his back. With the rest of the soldiers watching, the three men picked up Cassie's field litter and trotted to Black Hawk Two.

"Captain Jamison, this is Makleroy. Corporal Hong and I request permission to escort our patient to Fort Sill, Sir."

"Permission granted. Return to your units when the escort is over. Makleroy, keep us posted on her condition."

With a terse, "Roger that," Black Hawk Two lifted off.

*****

As Black Hawk Two exited the scene, Brian's pilot twisted the Sikorsky's collective and headed for the theater of operation.

Chapter Twenty-Four

Miles to the west, Stevens drove the deuce and a half over three consecutive sets of spike strips. All but one of the tires blew instantly. The truck turned into a wobbly, kid's go-cart on a cobblestone road. Stevens fought for control and slowed down to keep from tipping over. He careened the truck into a small turnout at the side of the road and nosed into the brush.

Seconds before, an Army Black Hawk had touched down on the highway and two soldiers had laid the strips. The Black Hawk landed and blocked the road fifty yards in front of the truck. A second Black Hawk had already landed and blocked the highway fifty yards behind the truck. The soldiers moved to a safe distance from the spike strips and waited for the truck to disable itself.

Stevens sat in the truck and waited. He wasn't disappointed that he hadn't reached Amarillo. He could set off the explosion and make his first political statement from here. The Major would be proud of him. The soldiers stayed back from the truck, just as The Major said they might. That was okay with Stevens. He didn't want to wait until they came closer. All he needed was enough time to set the timer and run far enough away from the truck.

Stevens reached for the door lever with his left hand. In the same motion, he reached down with his right hand and picked up the timer. With a last satisfied breath, he pressed the button. He counted to himself, reached for the door handle, and released the button.

Chapter Twenty-Five

Hong and the other medic covered Cassie with a heavy woolen blanket and finished strapping her into the transport gurney mounted on the Black Hawk's forward bulkhead. Hong inserted a saline IV. Black Hawk Two's pilot called Fort Sill Medical with an ETA and patient assessment.

Sergeant Makleroy sat in the helicopter jump seat without moving. He watched the two medics fuss over his charge with a bit of grateful bemusement. Hong checked the IV for the sixth time. The other medic adjusted the blanket for the eighth time. Both kept a running line of chatter focused on Cassie.

"Where're you from? Are you warm enough? How'd you find these guys? Are you breathing, okay? You're one badass Marine!"

Cassie did the best she could to keep up with answers. She wasn't incoherent, just groggy enough that she couldn't keep up with the conversation. She was only aware of her enjoyment in the warmth. Tonight was Cassie's second ride in a Black Hawk's gurney. This time was infinitely more comfortable. The first time had been during the Crucible.

*****

The Crucible is the final field exercise that a Marine recruit must survive at the end of their thirteen-week boot camp. It is a fifty-four-hour test of endurance, teamwork, and military skills. On the surface, the Crucible seems like a final test, but in reality, it's a time for the recruits to demonstrate to the Marines that they are qualified to represent the Marines and America around the world. It is also a time for the Marine Corps to demonstrate to the recruits that they were capable of far more than they imagined: they're capable of being Marines.

During fifty-four hours of the Crucible, the recruits get one four-hour sleep break and one-and-a-half MREs. An MRE is the equivalent of one dinner meal for the average civilian. The drill instructors issue the MREs at the start of the Crucible and the individual recruits must decide for themselves the most advantageous way to ration their limited food supply. The recruits spend the rest of the fifty-four hours taking part in thirty-two field training exercises, marching or double-timing between training exercises, and being ambushed or ambushing other training squads. The high level of physical exertion never lets up. Hunger sets in and is relentless. Even though the drill instructors try to keep the recruits hydrated, there are times when thirst becomes an issue. Of course, the heat and humidity of Paris Island are oppressive. Dirt, mud, and biting insects are everywhere.

During the Crucible, the DIs designate a different recruit to be in command in each of the training stations. The DIs provided all recruits the experience of taking command, evaluating a situation, and leading their squad through an obstacle at least twice. The ability of every Marine to step up and take command in any given situation is one of the most defining military traits of the Marines. Another defining trait of the Marines is their dedication to teamwork.

*****

Recruit Sing and her squad were in hour twenty of the Crucible when they marched into training station fourteen. Training station fourteen consisted of a thirty-foot-by-thirty-foot wood-framed box set in the ground. The box was full of sand and looked like a schoolyard sand box. The biggest truck tire that Recruit Sing had ever seen hung by chains from a fifteen-foot-tall, A-frame made of telephone poles. The apparatus looked like a giant child's swing set. The bottom of the opening in the tire was level with the recruits' shoulders. Two more ten-foot lengths of chain hung from the bottom of the tire at four o'clock and eight o'clock.

The drill instructor shouted, "Drop you packs and gear on the grass starting pad." Marines never let their weapons out of their possession. "Gather round," the drill instructor ordered. Twelve recruits slung their weapons over their shoulders and formed a tight circle near the drill instructor.

The DI pointed to a low ridge about a mile away and reported, "Alpha Company is under attack on the top of the next ridge. They are running low on ammo. Your assignment is to resupply Alpha Company. Before you leave, you will pass all recruits, your gear, packs, weapons and two ammo cans each (forty pounds each) through the tire without touching the tire. You will return anything or anybody that touches the tire to the grass staging area and start again. You will return anyone who touches the sand with any part of the body except your boots to the grass staging area and start again. You may move around to any side of the tire during the exercise whether you have passed through the tire or not. You may not touch the tire. Recruit Sing, you are in command of this exercise! You have your orders."

Recruit Sing took command. "Four recruits move to the other side of the tire. Davis and Smith, pass off your rifles. Pick up Davis and pass her through the tire."

Recruit Sing though, *this is too easy. Something's coming.*

She was right. The builders of the A-frame left considerable give in the joints. As the squad started to pass Recruit Davis though the tire, a DI pushed the side of the A-frame with her boot. The tire started to swing, and Davis touched the swinging tire. After a couple of attempts to synchronize their movements to the swinging tire and failing, Recruit Sing had an epiphany. Two more lengths of chain hung from the tire.

"Come on, recruits, move. Marines are dying on that ridge," The drill instructor screamed.

Recruit Sing shouted, "The drill instructor said that we couldn't touch the tire. She didn't say that we couldn't touch the chains. Two each, grab the lower chains and put your weight behind them. Hold the tire steady. Everybody else, start again." Once the recruits steadied the tire against the disruptive actions of the DI, the squad completed the exercise in minutes.

After they passed the equipment through the tire, Recruit Sing ordered, "Everybody, gear up, two ammo cans each! Double time at 10-foot defensive intervals to the ridge. Marines need resupply."

Before the first recruit could move a step, the drill instructor shouted, "Recruit Sing, you have just been wounded, a sucking chest wound." She slapped an adhesive X a little below Recruit Sing's collarbone.

Some of the recruits called, "Sniper," and hit the ground, turning to face the direction that Recruit Sing was facing. Recruit Lake was the last to move.

The drill instructor shouted, "Recruit Lake, you are too slow. You have a glancing gunshot to the head. Drop your helmet!"

A muted flash from a remotely operated strobe light appeared in the trees one hundred yards away. Most of the recruits fired blank shots in that direction. Two recruits rendered make-believe first aid to the wounded recruits.

The DI shouted, "The sniper is eliminated!"

The recruits formed a tight defensive circle and turned their attention to the designated wounded. Right on cue, a Black Hawk appeared out of the night and landed in the clearing next to the tire training pad. The recruits loaded their wounded. The helicopter dusted off.

Recruit Davis shouted, "Gear up, two ammo cans each. Double time to the ridge at ten-foot defensive intervals!"

The helicopter flight lasted less than a minute. The simulated wounded were ferried to the next training station. It was just over the ridge from the tire training station. During the flight, the Black Hawk crew left the recruits strapped to their gurneys. Recruit Sing had time to reflect on the events of the night. Everything seemed so real. They had ambushed other squads. Other squads had ambushed them. They had simulated gunfights and mortar attacks. Recruit Sing had experienced a gut-wrenching medevac helicopter extraction. The smell of the cordite was real. The recruits were hungry, thirsty, and sleep deprived. The only difference between this experience and real combat was that none of the recruits were hurt.

Recruit Sing acknowledged the reality that, for the military, training was bloodless war and war was bloody training.

The Black Hawk touched down and the recruits were ushered off the helicopter. A drill instructor met them.

"The objective of this station is to obtain four hours of sleep. Find your squad flag. When your squad arrives, lead them to your flag. This is a simulated combat zone. Act accordingly. In four hours, you will move out!"

Half an hour later, the rest of Recruit Sing's squad marched into the training station. Recruit Sing set up an impromptu duty roster. This being an active combat zone, Recruit Sing assigned a rotating roster for a stationary perimeter guard on the outer perimeter and a roaming fireguard on the inner perimeter. She assigned herself to the last time slot. If the drill instructors planned to pull a surprise attack on the squad, it would be in that last hour. The squad bedded down. The recruits were all asleep in minutes.

Recruit Sing's last thoughts before sleep were images of previous graduating companies of female Marines returning from the Crucible. She could see them running with exuberance. She could hear the echoes of grit in their singing. She thought how impossible that was going to be for this squad. They were all exhausted; they were mentally spent; they were hungry; and they were twenty hours into the Crucible. The recruits had thirty hours to go. Recruit Sing didn't know how they could have the energy required to run back to base in another day and a half.

She took a deep breath, closed her eyes, let her breath out slowly, and fell asleep. Like most recruits, Recruit Sing had developed the ability to fall asleep instantly, regardless of the activity level around her, and wake up fully alert after minimal sleep.

*****

Cassie became more coherent. The drugs were wearing off, and Cassie's side ached. They were halfway to Fort Sill, but Cassie asked if she could get another shot anyway. Hong smiled and said that he was sorry.

Chapter Twenty-Six

The Sikorsky made a cautious landing on a grassy knoll near the cabin and away from the main driveway. Brian stepped out of the bubble door and walked to the gravel parking lot. His silk suit was incongruous with the scene around him, which looked like a set out of a combat movie.

A man in a pilot's jumpsuit and helmet detached himself from the crowd of soldiers and approached Brian.

"Mr. Sing, Captain Jamison."

"My niece?"

"Sir, Lance Corporal Sing was wounded during an exchange of gunfire with the suspects. Her wounds aren't life-threatening."

The concussive report of an explosion startled everyone on the site. As one, they turned to the west where a fireball was transitioning from bright red to burnt orange. The deuce and a half was gone.

When the fireball was dark and the spectacle faded back into the night sky, Jamison continued, "We medevac'd her to the trauma center at the Fort Sill Base Hospital. She's in good hands and will be all right, Sir."

Brian turned and surveyed the scene before him as the words replayed through his thoughts, *an exchange of gunfire.* After a second, he turned to the two men lying face down on the ground.

"Are those our suspects?" Brian asked, indicating the two on the ground.

"Two of them, yes, Sir; there were seven. One drove the deuce and a half out of the compound some time ago. I suspect that fireball just consumed him. Lance Corporal Sing killed a second and took his weapon. My crewman took out a third as he was drawing down on Lance Corporal Sing. These two killed two others before we entered the cabin. These are the only two left."

"Get them up," Brian ordered.

Jamison nodded to his men.

The GIs pulled the remaining freedom fighters to their feet. Neither suspect displayed the confidence or bravado that they had over the last couple of days. Brian stepped so close to the first man that the dirt falling from the man's clothing landed on Brian's pants cuff and shoes.

"Has anyone read you your rights?"

The dirty man must have thought that the man in the silk suit was there to protect him because he smiled a little and said with a tinge of smugness, "Nobody read me my rights."

Brian's face didn't crack. "That's good. I'm arresting you under title VIII of the Patriot Act of 2001 which means that you have no rights. I'm personally going to see to it that you spend the rest of your natural life in the slinkiest shithole that I can find at Guantanamo Bay prison. Nobody but you and I are ever going to know what happened to you. Understand?"

The suspect's eyes were as wide as they could stretch. If he had any pee left, he would have wet his pants again.

"This soldier is going to ask you some questions. That soldier is going to ask your buddy the same questions. The first one who tells me what I want to know will get a six-inch-by-six-inch window in his cell."

Brian's stare didn't waver, and he was certain that the man understood his situation. He stepped over to the second suspect and repeated the offer. As Brian finished, Jamison motioned him to step aside and led him to the pole barn.

"We did a sweep. We didn't find any bombs or booby traps. I think that you should see the truck."

As Brian rounded the back of the truck, he understood Jamison's interest. One of the soldiers had removed both hinge pins. The small hatch was lying on the ground.

Jamison said, "Quite the little engineering project."

Brian could see the round end of one of the Styrofoam clamshells. He had to admit a little admiration for the cleverness of the design. Yes, the tank truck disguised the weapons quite well. But there was more. The Styrofoam was a natural radiation shield. The metal tube was a second layer of shielding, and the water in the larger tank was the perfect outer shield.

"A team of weapons specialists from Fort Sill is inbound with two transport trucks. We'll stand guard on the milk truck until they arrive. Then, it's their ball game."

Brian nodded. He didn't want to mess with the weapons either.

The materials around an unexploded nuclear weapon absorbed some of the radiation. Dissimilar materials absorbed different types of radiation in different ways. Each material in the truck would absorb different energies of ambient radiation. The layer of water was the best absorber. The water in the outside tank would absorb or change most of the remaining radiation signature. Brian had seen many nuclear spent fuel storage pits in his past jobs. The engineers responsible for reducing the amount of radiation exposure to workers would fill the spent fuel storage pits with water because it was such a natural radiation shield.

Every weapon in America's nuclear arsenal emitted its own spectra of radiations. Just as a person could be identified by his or her voiceprint, the class of a nuclear weapon could be identified by its radiation spectrum.

*****

Most American weapons detection equipment contain libraries of nuclear weapon spectrum profiles. A detection vehicle should pull up alongside a vehicle suspected of carrying a nuclear weapon and scan the spectrum. If the scan matches a known spectrum, there is high probability that the truck is carrying the weapon that matches that scan.

There is a reason for the spectrum comparison approach to weapons detection. A great many things are radioactive besides nuclear weapons. Bananas, grown in nature, are ever so slightly radioactive and have their own spectrum. A truckload of smoke detectors has a radiation spectrum. Coal and crude oil are two materials with a moderate natural radioactive signature that are transported on the road and rails in the United States.

*****

The design of the milk truck was ingenious. The materials used, especially the water, will alter and/or reduce the radioactive spectrum detected.

A vehicle-mounted nuclear weapons detection system might not even recognize the filtered spectrum. The computer might think the truck was carrying chemical fertilizer and pass it by.

Brian realized that if Cassie hadn't stopped this plot when she did, the drivers of the truck would have had a free pass to drive the nation's highways.

Brian was looking at the pile of shipping skeleton pieces discarded at the back of the pole barn. He was deep into the possible scenarios when Jamison touched his arm to get his attention.

"The cabin has a wealth of intelligence and documentation. The problem is that there's too much information for it to be accidental or random. They wanted us to find these clues. I have a theory."

"Tell me."

"Well, to start with, the GPS transponder in the deuce and a half came on about twenty minutes before we caught up with it. Even if Lance Corporal Sing hadn't alerted us to the deuce's location and cargo, we would have found the truck before it reached any metropolitan centers. The difference is that we would have approached the truck and would now have casualties. I think they meant for us to follow the truck on a wild goose chase, get caught in the explosion, and spin our wheels investigating that site instead of searching for this site.

"The recovered intel in the cabin all leads to a second location, an abandoned commercial building in the heart of Oklahoma City. Those two stooges confirm that they thought that the plan was to take the weapons to that site as a next destination.

Jamison paused to let the Brian absorb the information, then started again.

"As obvious as the plethora of clues is, I think that they meant it as a diversion. They expected us to go charging up to Oklahoma City while some of this crew drove off into the sunset with our weapons. They may have also wired the Oklahoma City site with explosives as they did the truck. We think that we were meant to spend time chasing phantoms up there, as well."

Jamison indicated the two suspects who were now sitting on the ground looking like scared puppies, "Those two have the same story. The group leader was one of the bodies in the cabin. He is wearing a fatigue jacket with the insignias of an Army major incorrectly placed on his jacket. A man called Flat Top was his second in command. Sergeant Makleroy, my lead crewman, took him out as we landed. Apparently, they were the only two who knew anything of any value. The other five here are wannabes: no real threat and no real Intel. As of right now, we don't know where the weapons were going, what they were going to be used for, or by whom."

Jamison paused again. When Brian looked at him again, he continued, "We did find one interesting piece of paper in the back pants pocket of one of the dead men in the cabin."

He gave the paper to Brian and said, "It's a nuclear weapon transfer authorization from Fourth Army Command Headquarters. It looks authentic. There is a withdrawal signature on the form that looks to me to be valid."

Brian took the paper and examined it. "May I take a picture of the form?" Brian knew that he couldn't remove evidence from an active crime scene.

"Well, that would be a felony, but yes, Sir, you can."

Brian took out his cell phone and snapped a picture of the form. He expanded the form to make sure that he could read the signatures. He wasn't concerned with the signature of the sergeant who released the weapons. He wanted the signature of the documents clerk who processed the request.

Satisfied, Brian asked, "You mentioned a site B in Oklahoma City. What's the address?"

Jamison produced another piece of paper that had an address handwritten across the bottom. Brian photographed it as well and then returned his phone to his pocket.

Jamison said, "We can finish processing this site, but we have no authority to proceed to Oklahoma City. That site is in civilian jurisdiction. I'm guessing that you can help pursue that lead?"

Brian nodded, smiled, stepped aside, and took out his cell phone. He didn't have the private number for the Oklahoma State Attorney General. Brian knew him but not well. So, he contacted the Oklahoma State switchboard operator, identified himself, and asked for an emergency transfer. He briefed the AG and asked for a joint operation to address the warehouse in Oklahoma City. Brian didn't abide surprising local law enforcement. He wanted the locals in the operation on the ground from the start even though DHS would be in charge.

Once Brian had the name of the AG's liaison, he conference-called the FBI Midwest Field Office, Agent in Charge of the FBI Terrorist Task Force and his aide at DHS. After briefing the task force leaders, he excused himself from the conversation, confident that the team would investigate and neutralize the Oklahoma City location.

Brian spent the rest of the morning with Jamison, investigating the intel at the cabin. He also monitored the removal and shipping of the two re-acquired warheads. Brian had a busy morning after a sleepless night. He, too, was getting tired.

Chapter Twenty-Seven

The Black Hawk with Cassie on board made a careful approach to the helipad at the Fort Sill Hospital. The regular triage reception team was waiting, surrounded by an entourage of other doctors, nurses, and hospital staff. Word about Cassie's exploit had spread quickly. Aside from the triage team, most of the staff wanted to be available in case they could help. A few just wanted to catch a glimpse of the Marine hero.

A group of two doctors and two nurses separated themselves from the crowd and pushed a wheeled gurney out to the Black Hawk's side door. The helicopter crew medics unstrapped Cassie's litter. They, and the two nurses, hefted Cassie out of the Black Hawk as the two doctors began their assessments. Sergeant Makleroy, with his rifle slung on his back, walked along behind the gurney. As the team hustled into the hospital, Hong recited the medical history of the patient as best as he could. Several other doctors peered over the team's shoulders. There were no obvious head wounds, so the neurosurgeon backed away. The chest seemed intact, so the cardio-thoracic surgeon stepped away.

Major David Gibbons, MD, Head of Orthopedics and his aide, Captain Timothy Nickolaus, MD, noticed the field splint on Cassie's arm. When there was a lull in the flow of information, Major Gibbons asked, "Corporal Hong, what's your assessment of the arm injury?"

"The arm injury looks like a through-and-through. The joint doesn't seem to be damaged. I splinted it to prevent any nerve or vascular damage."

Major Gibbons and Captain Nickolaus fell away from the rushing group of people. Gibbons decided that they would follow up at a more convenient time. If the attending didn't order X-rays of the elbow, he would. He also decided that they'd drop by her room on the ward and have a look at the elbow. Gibbons and Nickolaus both knew that complications to the joint, nerves, or with the body's blood supply could arise hours or days after a gunshot wound. Both orthopedic doctors were experienced combat surgeons. Along with dozens of other doctors and nurses at Fort Sill Hospital, they made Cassie's recovery a personal project.

When the medical entourage reached the double swinging door entrance to the tri-age center, one of the nurses blocked the door before the two medics or Makleroy could follow.

She said, "We'll take it from here. Let me show you to the waiting room. I promise that I'll keep you posted on her condition every half-hour."

She motioned for an orderly dressed in fatigues to show them the way. "There's coffee and maybe some doughnuts left. There's also a cafeteria one floor down. Please, if there's anything else that you need, feel free to ask the orderly." Without waiting for a response, she turned and entered the triage suite.

The abrupt end to the need for their assistance caught all three of them off guard, and the sudden inactivity stunned them. They didn't want to follow the orderly, but they also didn't know which way to turn. After a few seconds of looking at each other for instructions, they followed the waiting orderly. They were just turning the corner to enter the waiting room when two MPs stepped up and addressed Sergeant Makleroy.

"Excuse us, Sergeant, hospital protocol doesn't allow you to carry weapons in the hospital. May we take your weapon and check it into the armory, or will you come with us and check it in yourself?"

Sergeant Makleroy wasn't accustomed to having anyone ask him to surrender his weapon. After a startled second, he answered, "My weapon? Uh, sure, I'll turn it in. Lead the way."

He had mixed feelings about leaving the waiting room, but he was more uneasy about surrendering his rifle. He followed the MPs to the elevator.

This shouldn't take too long, he thought.

Medical staff swarmed around Cassie like locusts. A nurse removed her boots, and another cut her clothes away. Someone bathed the area around the wounds with Betadine and distilled water. A nurse replaced the manual blood pressure cuff with an automatic cuff and started the device. Yet another drew a thermometer across Cassie's forehead. The barrage of questions continued.

"Can you breathe, okay? Take a deep breath."

"Does this hurt?" Poke.

"Does this hurt?" Prod.

"Does this hurt?" Someone pushed on the right side of Cassie's abdomen.

"Can you feel this?" Someone dragged a blunt object down the length of her left forearm and hand. "Any numbness?"

"Yes. No. No. Yes. No."

The triage doctor stepped away and a phlebotomist stepped in to draw blood. The doctor ordered, "I want an ultrasound of her abdomen. Do her left arm while you're at it. She doesn't seem to be in any distress. I want her vitals every fifteen minutes. He turned to Cassie and asked, "Are you awake enough to understand me?"

Cassie nodded.

"Good. Looks to me like you're in decent shape for a gunshot victim. I've ordered an ultrasound just to make sure that there are no hidden injuries inside. I don't like surprises. If all goes well, you should be up and around by dinner."

Cassie knew that he was joking, trying to bolster her spirits. She smiled at the doctor and said, "Thank you."

A nurse gave Cassie a tranquilizer. Cassie didn't mind some painkillers, but she hated drugs that messed with her mental capacities. For a few moments, Cassie fought the effects of the tranquilizer, but ultimately, she relaxed and almost fell sleep. The rest of the morning and half of the afternoon were more of the same and passed in a blur.

For the first ninety minutes that Cassie was at the Fort Sill Army Hospital, she had more doctors, nurses, medical technicians, orderlies, and support staff focused on her than the President of the United States did during his last physical at the Bethesda Naval Hospital in Maryland.

Chapter Twenty-Eight

Police Lieutenant Robert Minor called the briefing to order. In front of him were eight members of the Oklahoma City Special Weapons And Tactics team (SWAT), three DHS agents, and five agents from the FBI Tactical Operations Team. They were meeting in the tactical briefing room of the Main Street office of the Oklahoma City Police Department, five blocks from the abandoned target building. All the men wore a full complement of tactical assault gear.

"Gentlemen, we have intel of the highest reliability that a homegrown terrorist cell is operating out of a derelict building on West Reno Avenue. Homeland Security has asked us to investigate the site and to detain anyone found in the building as a possible terrorist. They have also advised us to operate with extreme caution. This group has already exploded one suicide bomb and may have placed explosive devices in the building. The authorities also suspect members of this group in the killing of two Army Military Policemen.

"Normally, we'd deploy one tactical team to drop down by rope onto the roof and deploy a second team to perform a street-level assault. Because we know that this group is willing to use explosives, we want to get in quick and secure all occupants before one of them has an opportunity to trigger an explosive. DHS has also requested that we keep the operation invisible to the public, if possible. That means a covert entry to secure as many of the occupants as possible before they detect our presence. The same goes for the press and news teams. We want to get in, complete the mission, and get out without being noticed.

"With that agenda in mind, we caught a break. We did a very public SWAT entry on the abandoned building next door to our target building this last winter to eliminate a meth lab. Now, it seems that in the recent past, the building next door was home to a furniture business. The owner of the furniture business obtained permission from the two building owners to open an access between the two buildings on the fourth floor to expand the space he had available for storing his inventory. To complete the operation last winter, we entered today's target building, crossed the fourth-floor access, and dropped down in the middle of the meth lab before they had time to react.

"Today, we'll reverse the process. Unfortunately, we can't enter the building without some measure of visibility to anyone watching from our target building. The building on the other side of the furniture store is occupied and open for business. That third building also has a street entrance around the corner from our target building. The owner has agreed to allow us to access his roof via his building for our operation."

Minor pointed to a rough map drawn on a white board behind him. "For today's operation, we'll enter this building through this entrance. We'll go to the roof and cross over to the abandoned furniture store–here. We'll descend to the fourth floor, reopen the modified access, if necessary, and cross into our target building. Lastly, we'll descend into the building and neutralize suspects as we find them. As I said, our secondary objective is to complete the operation without the public becoming aware.

"I want to reemphasize that this group has used bombs. Watch for booby-traps, trip wires, laser triggers, etc. Any questions?"

A hand went up, "Will we approach and withdraw using impounded civilian vehicles?"

"Yes. However, our tactical vehicles will be standing by in this alley, here." Minor pointed to the diagram and then looked around the room.

"If there are no more questions, saddle up. There are four vehicles in the basement staging area. Gentlemen, come back in one piece, that's an order."

*****

As the joint tactical team walked to their vehicles, Mitsy Walker, a twenty-two-year-old paralegal for Hawkins & Deering Law Firm, picked up her purse to leave the office for lunch. She couldn't pass up a chance to walk to her favorite Jewish deli on West Reno Avenue on a day like today. The spring sun was just too inviting. The streets were still wet from a brief morning shower. Mitsy could smell the odor of city life. In the summer, street performers would swarm the waterfront park. Today, however, the a few people out worked in the area.

Mitsy saw the sign for the deli a block and a half down West Reno. She didn't notice the panel-sided bread truck turning away from her at the corner and pulling up to the curb at the first business on the right. Or if she did, it didn't register. As the truck parked, three members of the SWAT team appeared for the briefest moment and darted into the building. The truck pulled away from the curb. Had Mitsy been looking in the direction of the unloading operation, she would have been alarmed at the sight of three heavily armed men in body armor moving with such purpose on a city street so near her. Mitsy continued to walk to the deli, relishing every step.

*****

With the last three members of the assault team on site, the team turned as one, strung out in single file, and climbed to the building's roof. A minute later, they were crossing to the roof of the abandoned furniture store. The first member of the SWAT team, SWAT One, dropped his laser filter glasses down over his face. The lenses made any laser beams visible. SWAT Two dropped his low-light night-vision binoculars into place. He was looking for trip wires. Both men grabbed the broken roof access door and pried it away from the frame. In a rush of hushed footsteps, the whole team descended to the fourth floor.

The access between the two buildings was still open and debris-free. SWAT One and SWAT Two scanned the fourth-floor room in the target building. Nothing seemed out of the ordinary. SWAT Two pointed to the floor. Five years of accumulated dust was undisturbed. No one had been in here recently.

SWAT Two thought, *they didn't check out the rest of their hideout? They didn't find a gaping backdoor to the middle of their nest. They didn't post a guard or even set an alarm. This is too easy.*

SWAT Three and SWAT Four peeled off and withdrew into the available cover to guard and secure the access corridor. They were the first two members of the rear guard. As the team descended, SWAT team members checked each floor for possible bogies hiding in the piles of junk on the upper floors. SWAT One, SWAT Two, and eight other members of the team descended to the ground floor.

*****

Seven members of The Major's Constitutional Reform Brigade were on the ground floor. They had done a half-assed job of securing the building. They had one man watching out the front window for any suspicious movement. One man patrolled the alley outside an open alley door. They believed that one loud call would be enough to alert the rest of the group if anyone tried to assault their hideout by the alley. The rest of the group lounged or slept in the main room.

The last known owner had turned off the electricity and water. A battery-operated radio broadcast the local news in the background. The group was listening for any news of the other half of their operation. The lack of air conditioning wasn't a noticeable inconvenience until later in the day. The cool night air kept the building comfortable for most of the morning. The men had packed a small, abandoned refrigerator with ice and stocked the remaining space with non-alcoholic drinks. They were enjoying the last few minutes of quiet. The Major and the other half of their brigade were due any minute. After that, the whole constitutional militia group would be too busy orchestrating the coming revisions to the government to get much rest.

The SWAT team was in place. With a hand mirror, SWAT Two watched one of the militiamen, Militia One, get off his dirty recliner and head for the refrigerator in the other room. Another militiaman, Militia Two, also got up and went to the bathroom, which didn't work because there was no water. That was okay, urine ran down the drain just fine.

Militia One was out of sight of the others as he opened the refrigerator. He took a carton of orange juice off the top shelf and drew a long drink from the open carton. He lowered the carton and his eyes met SWAT Nine's tinted goggles and the business end of an automatic rifle. From behind Militia One, the disembodied voice of SWAT Eleven whispered close to Militia One's ear, "Don't make a sound. Don't move."

A hand gloved in black fire-retardant material reached from behind Militia One, took the orange juice carton out of his hand, and placed it on the top of the refrigerator. The same hand placed a strip of tape over Militia One's mouth.

"You will be silent."

The threat of consequences was implied. SWAT Nine and SWAT Eleven slowly and quietly led Militia One to a quiet corner behind the SWAT team's forward line. Militia One was subdued.

Militia Two finished in the bathroom and stepped out of the open bathroom door. There was no need for modesty with this bunch of men. As he took his second step past the bathroom door, the walls on either side of him came alive. Suddenly, he had two assault rifles pointed at him. He decided that there was nowhere to run and no chance of getting there, so he opened and raised his hands. SWAT Four taped his mouth. SWAT Twelve and SWAT Thirteen pulled his arms behind his back, careful not to touch his un-washed hands, and plastic-cuffed him. They led Militia Two into the back rooms.

Militia Three milled around just out-side the back door. He thought he heard a sound, like an animal was scratching on the other side of the open door. There it was again. He stepped closer to the open door and whispered, "Is…"

He didn't get past the first word be-fore a Taser hit him. He went down with an audible grunt. Two SWAT team members pulled him into the darkness in the corner of the loading dock. Three were in custody, four to go.

The SWAT team also took Militias four and five without incident. The team was watching Militia Six and waiting for an op-portunity when Militia Six sprang up in alarm and said, "Hey, where is everybody?"

The team's secret was out. The remai-ning two militiamen were alarmed. Five members of the SWAT team burst into the room at the same instant.

They all made as much noise as possible, shouting, "Hands up!" and "Get down on the floor!" Several members turned on their red targeting lasers to add to the confusion.

The surprise was complete. Neither Militia Six nor Militia Seven had time to draw their next breath, much less a weapon. SWAT team members threw them to the floor and pinned them down. The only sound made by any of the militiamen made was Militia Seven's whimpered mew, "Okay, okay, okay, don't hurt me…"

On the street outside, an older woman walking her German Shepard and a teenage boy walking a black lab stopped practiced purpose and turned toward the nearest door of the building. They were both police bomb-sniffing canine units. They started their sweep for explosives at the doors and searched in an ever-widening circle. A member of the SWAT team accompanied each canine officer for the search of the rest of the building. After the teams cleared the first floor, they moved up the stairs. When the canine teams moved to the upper floors, a small army of forensic technicians set up shop on the ground floor.

As the new arrivals worked, the SWAT team prepared the suspects for transportation to the FBI headquarters for interrogation. The officers flex-cuffed each militiaman's hands in front of his body. The flex-cuffs had an extra one-inch plastic loop between the wrists. The officers pulled a second tether between the suspects' legs from back to front, threaded it through the loop on the wrist cuffs, and pulled the end of the tether down to the ankles. The tether also had a flex-cuff on the bottom end. The second tether was flex-cuffed to the ankle. The other end of the tether, the one behind the suspect's back, had a gripping loop on the end.

When Militia Seven was tethered, the escorting SWAT officer took a firm grip on the loop, placed a hand on the suspect's back, and moved him toward the alley door. It didn't take long for Militia Seven to realize that any resistance on his part would be painful. If he took one step away from his escort, the SWAT member could pull the gripping loop, tightening the tether, and pull his hands to his crotch, holding them there. It would be difficult to defend oneself, much less mount an attack, when he couldn't move his hands away from his zipper. Militia Seven also figured that if he took a second step away from his escort, the tether would have tightened even further and lifted his tethered ankle off the ground. Not only could he not defend himself, but he'd also fall in a spectacular way if he resisted. Most suspects accepted that disobedience would result in pain.

SWAT Seven put on an oversized sports logo jacket over his uniform and gear and concealed his weapons. They were just two employees walking out the back door of an abandoned building.

A different side-panel truck stopped next to the alley door. The truck had the markings and logo of a local plumbing service. A female agent opened the side door, and SWAT Seven stepped his new friend up to the truck and helped him into the back. The two agents hard-cuffed the militiaman to a ring hanging from the far wall. SWAT Seven followed his suspect into the back of the truck.

The female agent put her face next to the militiaman's, smiled hard, and asked, "Comfy?"

Another SWAT team member repeated the process with another militiaman. The female agent closed the sliding door. The truck left the alley and two of the suspects were on their way to a new way of life. The process was repeated three more times. The interrogations would begin at once.

The driver of the last transport truck stopped at the end of the alley. He turned right onto West Reno Avenue like an old lady coming home from church but had to stop for a traffic light at the end of the block. While he waited for the light to change, he couldn't help but notice the serenity of the scene around him. There weren't many people on the street, but the people who were there didn't seem to have a care in the world.

Take that young woman walking so carefree on the other side of the street: she carried a small lunch bag from the deli on the next block and, he guessed, *walking back to wherever she worked.*

Ironic, the driver thought. *She has no idea how close she was to a terrorist takedown operation today.*

She enjoyed the spring sun without a care because she didn't know who he had in the back of his potato chip delivery truck. She felt safe. She was safe. He was going to continue to try to preserve the secure feeling she felt right now for every day of her life.

The agent wondered how many other teams carried out takedown operations like this every day that the American public didn't know about. How many other threats did American authorities neutralize without costing the average American one minute of lost sleep? If he had been a betting man, he would have guessed dozens. The public just didn't need to know all the sordid secrets that Homeland Security kept out of public concern.

With a start, the driver realized that he had been staring at the young woman a little too long, and she was staring back. *That isn't how someone conducts himself when he's trying to stay inconspicuous.* The driver turned his gaze back to the traffic light and was surprised to find it was green. Without looking at the young woman again, he engaged the clutch and continued his drive to FBI headquarters.

*****

Mitsy was serene. It was such a perfect day. She stopped at a red light on the corner and pushed the pedestrian waiting button. When her attention turned to the potato chip truck stopped at the light, she realized that the driver was staring at her. It wasn't a creepy stare. The driver looked pleasant enough. She thought he must have liked what he saw. She lifted the corner of her mouth into a smile, but he looked away.

Wait, she thought, *I might be some-body that you'd like to get to know. You might be somebody that I'd like to get to know.*

The driver was striking. He appeared to be of Native American descent, had high cheekbones, a strong jaw, blue-black hair, and intelligent eyes. He was also pulling away down the street.

Wait, go around the block, come back by, and ask me for my phone number. Wait!

He didn't turn back around. He kept going and, within seconds, disappeared into traffic.

That was strange--nice but strange.

Mitsy knew that she was attractive, and she liked having men notice her. She was flattered to the point of being flustered. The five-second chance encounter made her day. It was icing on the top of an already relaxing lunchtime walk. Mitsy continued walking toward her office, but now she had a little more flirt in her smile and a little more *sexy* in her step.

What a perfect day.

Chapter Twenty-Nine

At 3:30 in the afternoon, a nurse walked Cassie back into her room. The pain in her side in her side was a background annoyance and the elbow was considered a minor wound. She was still a bit out of touch with planet hospital from the various drugs. She looked down at her left arm. The doctors had removed the splint and wrapped her arm from mid-forearm to mid upper arm. She flexed her elbow. The joint was stiff, and the soft tissues were sore, but the arm seemed to move normally. She flexed and fisted her hand. At first, the hand seemed unaffected. Cassie had just stroked her fingertips across the palm of her hand when a nurse asked, "How's the arm?"

"It seems fine, a little sore and stiff, but fine."

"And the side?"

"It's not as sore."

The nurse smiled and nodded. "Your doctor put in your chart that might clear you for release tomorrow and for return to light duty in five days. We're all pretty impressed."

Cassie noticed the unusual number of people in the hall, and they were all watching her. Others stepped out of open office doorways as she went by. Cassie looked at the nurse and raised her brows.

"You're something of a celebrity. Everybody's curious. You brought down an armed radical militia group single-handedly?"

Cassie flushed and said, "I was involved, but I didn't do it alone. A lot of soldiers did the heavy lifting. Was anyone else injured?"

"Nope. You'll have to tell me the whole story later. They're all going to accost me when I leave your room in a few minutes. Here we are."

They turned into Cassie's room. She saw three men in fatigues standing in the hall across from her room.

The nurse leaned down and said, "They're the medics and infantryman that brought you in. They wouldn't leave."

Cassie stole another glance and waved at them before she went through the door. The nurses tried to help get into bed, but Cassie did most of the work herself. She couldn't put any pressure on her left arm, and she pretended that her left side didn't hurt much. The nurses arranged her blankets, her pillows, her IV, and her call button. Finally, a

272

nurse rolled a meal table over the top of her lap. An obligatory pitcher of ice water was on the table. Cassie was curious about the dozen, or so small Jell-O containers and another dozen cans of mixed fruit flavored juices. Again, Cassie looked quizzical.

"The doctor ordered a liquid diet for the rest of the day. These have been coming in from well-wishers all afternoon. Keep them down and it is solid food for dinner."

"That's good. I'm starving."

"Can I order you anything else? Coffee, tea, broth maybe?"

"Yes, please, coffee black and broth. Will you ask if the kitchen will mix the broth half chicken and half beef?"

The fifty-fifty mixed broth was the secret to Cassie's homemade egg drop soup.

"Your Uncle Brian called and said to tell you that he'd be in later. He had some cleanup business to take care of. Your Aunt Lenell called and said she'd try later, but to call her if you can. Your parents said that they'd call back later, and your commanding officer called. I promised to call him as soon as you were in your room. Are you ready to receive guests?"

Cassie wasn't sure, but she said, "Sure," anyway.

The nurse stepped to the door and nodded to the men outside. "Lance Corporal Sing, this is Sergeant Makleroy, Corporal Hong, and Corporal Lake." She turned to the three visitors and said, "Ten minutes, no more!"

The four of them made quick introductions. Each gave a short recounting of their part in the recovery of the weapons.

"Well, you're sure look better."

"How are you feeling?"

"Good shooting."

"Oorah!"

"How'd you get out there in the first place?"

"Are you going to have a good battle scar?"

Cassie gave a synopsis of her evening.

"Oorah!"

Cassie stayed involved with the conversation, but her attention kept going back to her left hand. Earlier, Cassie noticed that the little finger on her left hand was numb. It had no sensation of cold from the cup of ice water that she was holding. While the small group regaled stories of the evening, Cassie used the nub of a pen to stimulate the skin on her hand.

The little finger of her left hand was numb. So was the outside half of the ring finger. A third of the palm of her hand below the two fingers and a small triangular wedge on the outside of her forearm also had no sensation to touch. She flexed her hand, and it moved okay. She tested the strength of her hand. Her fingers were plenty strong. Only the nerves in the skin seemed to be involved. If she stroked the skin lightly, she felt nothing. If she pressed the pen a little harder, she could feel the pressure deep in the surrounding soft tissues of her hand.

Cassie decided not to say anything to the doctors. After all, the loss of feeling might just be temporary. She was taking no chances. She didn't know what kind of disability, however minor, might render her medically unfit for service. She had heard that flat feet, color blindness, and high blood pressure had all led to a Marine's discharge. Cassie wasn't willing to risk that the Marines might not consider the numbness minor.

The four swapped stories and laughed at each other's attempts at humor. Cassie stroked her left hand with the fingertips of her right hand, trying to get used to the sensation.

The floor nurse walked back into the room carrying a tray with several large Styrofoam cups on it and said, "Okay, everybody out. You can come back tomorrow. It's time for some nurse work. C'mon, gentlemen, out, out, out."

She turned to Cassie. As she set the cups on Cassie's rollaway tray, she identified each cup, "Coffee, beef broth, chicken broth, and an empty cup so you can mix your own. The kitchen staff also sent you this." She put a bottle of Perrier on the tray. "I don't think that it'll hurt anything."

A second nurse walked in carrying two extra pillows and asked, "Lance Corporal Sing?"

"Call me Cassie."

"Cassie, my name is Lucy. I come on the night shift at five o'clock. I'll come by later and get some vitals. How are you doing this afternoon? Any pain?"

The next tech through the door announced, "Good afternoon, Corporal Sing. My name is Merci. Your doctor ordered physical therapy for you every hour on the hour if you expect to return to light duty tomorrow. So, it's time to walk the halls. Let me help you up."

She dropped the side rail and locked it down.

"I think I can get up on my own."

Using the side rail for leverage, Cassie locked her ankles together and sat up. She sat for a few seconds then swung her legs over the edge of the bed and stood up.

"I'm a bit lightheaded. Do you have a walker?"

The stream of medical personnel continued all afternoon, some on business, some paying respects, and some just curious.

Chapter Thirty

Susan Wajowski walked the drab, basil-green hallway back to her office, her afternoon stack of transfer documents duly processed and distributed. Her building was a sixty-year-old relic of the cold war and smelled as much. The military police had lifted the security shutdown several hours earlier. There was no word about what caused the base lockdown, even in the base scuttlebutt. She knew that she wouldn't hear from Flea until the operation was completed. So, to Susan, no news was good news. It was almost 3:30 p.m. and Susan was more than ready to head home. This had been one of the most stressful days of her life.

She turned down the small side corridor to her office. The inadequate lighting pulled the ambiance down further. Her closet-sized office was the last door on the right. She unlocked and opened her door, then stopped. There were three men in her office. Two Marines were in class A Khaki uniforms and were obviously military police on official business. Both were well over six feet tall, intimidating, menacing. They meant to be. Neither smiled nor greeted her.

The third man was smaller, older, and wearing a dark suit. He carried an air of authority and command. In violation of several classified document protocols, he was holding one of her transfer documents and comparing it to an image on his cell phone.

When Susan walked in, he put the transfer order that he had been holding back in her out basket.

"Susan Wajowski, ex-wife of Teddy Wajowski?" He didn't smile.

"Yes."

"My name is Brian Sing. I'm with the Department of Homeland Security."

Chapter Thirty-One

By eighteen-thirty hours, 6:30 p.m., Doctors Gibbons and Nickolaus were back. Cassie had just returned from her latest therapeutic hike around the hospital's main hall. Dr. Gibbons rolled and flexed Cassie's arm for the third time.

"Any pain in the joint here, here, or here? Squeeze my hand, any weakness in your grip?" He ran his pen down the middle of Cassie's palm. "You can feel that?"

He didn't test for feeling in Cassie's two outside fingers. Dr. Nickolaus was opening his mouth to inquire about the exercises that the therapist assigned for the elbow when an Army Captain entered the room and ordered, "Attention!"

Major General Omar Marks, Commanding Officer, Fourth Army Command, followed the captain into the room and said, "As you were, as you were. Be at ease, especially you, Corporal Sing. Relax."

All activity in the room stopped except for General Marks's. General Marks's presence in the room eclipsed the presence of everyone else, and he expected no less.

"I've been trying to get down here all afternoon and check on you. How're you doing? You look amazingly well. Are you sure that you've been shot?"

Cassie held up her arm and said, "Yes, Sir."

"Yes, of course. I've been hearing some spectacular stories about your ordeal last night. I'll bet some of them are true, too. Did you really take down a seven-man, home-grown terrorist cell and recover two stolen nuclear weapons single-handedly?"

Again, Cassie clarified the events, "I was involved, Sir, but there were a lot of soldiers, pilots, medics and one civilian active in the take down. I didn't do it alone."

"Well, I can't wait to read your full report. Sounds like the makings of a good movie."

General Marks paused a moment, relaxed a bit, leaned in, and asked, "You really are doing as well as you seem to be? They're taking good care of you here?"

Cassie gestured that they were.

General Marks reached into a shirt pocket and took out a business card. He flipped it over and started writing something on the back. As he wrote, he asked, "How's your family holding up. You've called them, right?"

He didn't wait for any answers.

"Here's my business card. That's my personal cell phone number on the back. If you or your family needs anything, any assistance whatsoever, any wheels greased, you call me personally, understand? I mean it, call me. I understand that your Uncle Brian is in the area investigating this incident. Ask him to give me a call. I'll treat him to a round of golf at the Fort Sill course over on Medicine Creek.

"Make sure these doctors take good care of you. Don't let them deny you anything. I understand that you're on an all-liquids diet. Well, Scotch is a liquid. If you want a double Scotch toddy, just order it. If they say no, call me. In my estimation, you've earned it."

The general laughed at his humor. Of course, everyone else laughed as well. The doctors were relieved when the general laughed. They didn't want to have to give a surgical patient an alcoholic beverage in the hospital.

General Marks softened even more as he looked Cassie in the eyes. He lowered his voice, put a measure of admiration in his tone, and said, "You did yourself proud, Marine. You did the Marine Corps proud. Well done, well done."

General Marks nodded, straightened his stance, and headed to the door. The captain called everyone to attention. The general spoke as he walked, "Get better, Marine. The Corps needs you. Don't forget, you or your family need anything, you call me."

The room returned to normal. The presence of the other occupants returned. Collectively, they all took a deep breath. Then Dr. Gibbons turned to Cassie and said, "No, you can't have a double Scotch today. Have some beef bouillon. We'll check in on the progress of your therapy in the morning. Your doctor plans to release you to limited duty tomorrow afternoon. I'll co-sign your discharge papers when I get back to my office."

Cassie nodded. Doctors Gibbons and Nickolaus left. As the nurses took yet another set of vitals, Cassie examined the business card. An Army logo, the American flag, and the flag of the Fourth Army Command were on the front. General Marks's name and title were embossed in gold. Below the name, a list of phone numbers and email addresses attested to how easy it was to contact General Marks.

Cassie flipped the card over, and General Marks had indeed written his cell phone number on the back. Next to the phone number, General Marks had sketched a simple emoticon. It had a typical round face, but its eyes were stern, and the mouth formed a growl. General Marks had added a Marine Corps eight-pointed cover on the emoticon.

The card might have seemed like just another business gesture to most people, but not to Cassie. The events of last night were Cassie's first real call to duty. She faced an enemy of her nation and chose to protect her fellow citizens. She wasn't flying a fighter jet along the North Korean coastline or carrying a rifle in Iraq, but she stood her post with honor. As the general said, she "did herself proud."

The business card was the first token of appreciation given to her in recognition of her bravery and service. To Cassie, the card was so much more. The card was a token of personal recognition straight from the hands of a general. It was her first medal, so to speak. Cassie held the card as though it was made of solid gold. Looking at the card answered so many of the questions she had about her life.

The nurse announced that it was time for Cassie to walk the halls. Cassie got out of bed without assistance, stowed the card in her personal belongings, and started walking. She decided that on this trip she'd try not to use the cane for the entire loop around the main floor.

Chapter Thirty-Two

By twenty hundred hours, the stream of doctors, nurses, medical technicians, counselors, command officers, well-wishers, chaplains, and curious had tapered off. Cassie was alone and resting quietly. Her side hurt, but she maintained her stony game face. Even though Cassie was injured and in a hospital bed, she still represented The United States, the Marine Corps, and herself. She couldn't let go of her game face or the heightened state of readiness.

Cassie was in a slight daze of stress and fatigue. She was staring at the knobs on the television, more asleep than awake. She wouldn't have been able to tell anyone the subject of the current news story.

Uncle Brian walked into the room.

"Hey," he said quietly, "are you receiving guests?"

"I am," she answered and added the smallest of smiles. "Come in. How are you?"

"You know me; I'm always good, *Sadaa Adarsh*. The question is how are you? You've had quite an eventful last twenty-four hours?" Brian started to sit in a chair next to the wall.

"No, sit up here. I can't see you down there," Cassie said with a wave of her hand to indicate the side of the bed.

For Cassie, the change was palpable. For the first time since boot camp, she wasn't all *Marine*. She let the obligation slip a notch. Lance Corporal Sing gave way to Cassie. She breathed heavier and was relieved to see her uncle.

Brian took Cassie's good hand in his and looked with exaggerated admiration at the soft wrap on the other arm.

"Are you going to have an impressive scar? Have you called your mother to let her know that you are good?"

Brian looked at Cassie, but he didn't see a wounded Marine in a base hospital. He saw his six-year-old niece playing in their backyard pool. She would always be six years old. Brian saw a child in a full Marine Corps combat uniform, sitting in a wading pool.

"I called Mama this afternoon. She wanted to fly out of here, but I told her that I would be out of the hospital and back to light duty before she could get here. Besides, she knew that you were in the area and would watch out for me." Lance Corporal Sing dropped further back into her role as Cassie.

"Have you been hearing stories about what happened?"

"Some. Thanks to you, the truck driver was the one casualty when the truck blew up. We recovered both nukes. That's gotta make today a good day, right?" Cassie's eyes showed her relief. Her emotions needed to come out. Her ordeal was over, and it was time to release the negative emotions of last night.

Brian didn't notice Cassie's tears at first. He kept talking and tried to stay light-hearted.

"We have nine in custody. We captured seven suspects at an abandoned warehouse in Oklahoma City. We found two alive and four dead at the hunting cabin. Their own men killed two in the cabin. We arrested the ex-wife of one of the suspects a couple of hours ago. She supplied the document that allowed the theft in the first place.

"We've questioned the live suspects and profiled the background of all fourteen men. Our conclusion is that none of them had the sophistication to use the weapons that they stole. They were either going to pass them on or sell them. We haven't found any evidence to lead us to any other people or organizations. The two leaders, The Major and Flat Top, both died at the cabin."

Cassie pulled on Brian's hand. When he was close enough, she put her good arm around his neck and cried.

"I'm sorry," she said and pulled away. "I'm sorry. I don't know what came over me. Marines don't cry."

Brian held tighter to her hug. "Sure, they do. It's a normal stress reaction. You need to let it out. It's good for you to let it out." He held her a little tighter. "You just go ahead and have as long a cry as you want. I'm not going anywhere."

That's what Cassie did. She let it all go. A few minutes later, when her tears had dried, she was spent. She was exhausted to her core. She needed to sleep. The last time she felt this exhausted was at the end of the Crucible in the final week of boot camp.

*****

On the morning of the third day of the Crucible, the two companies of female recruits reformed into one unit and were walking back to the main camp, single file at ten-yard intervals. It was up to each recruit to keep an interval of ten yards between her and the recruit in front of her. Recruit Sing had thought the Crucible might be over, but, if the Marine Corps had driven anything into her brain, it was to never assume anything. The unexpected would always happen. She kept her focus on the terrain on either side of the walking column. The DIs wouldn't catch Recruit Sing napping today.

The column of recruits walked along the road that connected the Paris Island main base with the Crucible training area. Recruit Sing was happy that the ordeal was over, but she couldn't let down her guard. As she rounded a bend in the road, she saw that the head of the column had veered off the road and onto a dirt turnout. Alpha Company had formed four ranks. They marched in place until both companies had completed the formation. Of the original ninety-six recruits, ten had dropped out during the three months of training. None had dropped out during the Crucible. Eighty-six were still in the program, forty-two in Alpha Company, and forty-four in Bravo Company. Recruit Sing could see a raised wooded platform against the tree line next to the recruit formation.

What now? What more could they want from us?

Recruit Sing hurt all over. She knew she had blisters on her feet and her left foot had a bruise across the top from an ammo can. Her ankles were stiff from constant walking without adequate rest. Her calf muscles were sore and cramping. Whenever she stopped, her thighs trembled from overexertion. Recruit Sing's right knee concerned her the most. She thought that she had a sprain. It was painful to walk. All the recruits were grimy. The humidity mixed the dirt with sweat and made sticky mud in all the bodies' creases. She could feel the sand in her hair. Her canvas belt rubbed gouges into her hips. The front straps of her field pack chafed new raw places over the old raw places. She was growling hungry. The meager MRE allotment hadn't lasted long enough or been satisfying enough. The one discomfort that Recruit Sing wasn't experiencing was thirst. The DIs had insisted that the recruits stay hydrated. Recruit Sing had half a canteen of water. She knew that all the other recruits were in the same condition, but no one could tell by looking at them. They looked strong, fit, and ready for anything. Recruit Sing contributed to the image by mentally reciting a mantra: *don't limp, don't limp, you wimp, don't limp.* At that moment, Recruit Sing couldn't imagine having the strength or the willpower to run back to the base.

Alpha Company was marching in place. As the last Bravo Company recruits filed into the formation, the senior drill instructor mounted the wooden platform. She called for order.

"Battalion!"

The company drill instructors shouted, "Company!"

The senior drill instructor finished her order by adding, "Halt!"

The company drill instructors shouted, "Halt!"

Recruit Sing added a mental, *Right step, left step, stop.*

The senior drill instructor ordered, "Right…face!"

The recruits turned as one and faced the platform. Recruit Sing's thighs trembled. The recruits held their weapons at port arms, across their chests with their right hands on the stock and left hands on the barrel.

The senior drill instructor ordered, "Order… arms!"

The recruits lowered their weapons alongside their right legs with the butts of the weapons on the ground by their right feet and their left hands wrapped around the weapons' sights. The recruits still stood at attention.

The senior drill instructor gave a non-standard order, "Recruits, drop your gear to the ground on your left side. Place your weapons on top of your gear."

Recruit Sing followed the orders and then returned to attention. She noticed that an unusual number of DIs had joined their formation.

The senior drill instructor shouted, "At ease. Give me your attention up here. Ninety-one days ago, ninety-six civilians entered Marine Corps Recruit Processing Command at Paris Island. Over the course of those ninety-one days, ten recruits dropped out. Fifty-four hours ago, the remaining eighty-six well-trained Marine recruits marched to their final test in the Crucible. I'm pleased to say that not one of your numbers dropped out during the Crucible. That is a testament to your ability to work together as a military unit, as a team, to complete your mission. We stay the course together. Oo-rah!"

The recruits roared, "Oorah!" Recruit Sing was beginning to feel better.

"Your drill instructors are passing out your new Marine insignia: the Eagle, Globe, and Anchor. You will hold them until ordered to install them.

"The Eagle, with outspread wings, is the symbol of our proud nation. America is a land of justice and freedom. The Eagle is reluctant to make war, but ever ready to fight for the freedom for oppressed people.

"The Globe, with the western hemisphere showing, is a symbol of the commitment of the U.S. Marines to serve anywhere in the world where our country needs our representation. It is a symbol of the area covered by Marines in service.

"The Anchor is symbolic of the close association between U.S. Marine Corps and U.S. Navy, on whose ships Marines have fought with honor and valor. The anchor is also a symbol of steadfast faithfulness, even unto death. Marines have always defended American principles, ideals, citizens, and territories.

"The rope entwined about the anchor is a braided rope. Both rope and anchor were part of the original embroidered patch. The eagle and globe were secured to the emblem in a later revision. Fouled anchors originate with the British Royal Navy, who used them on common naval buttons.

"Before you affix your insignias, Chaplain Masterson will lead us in prayer."

As Chaplain Masterson stepped to the front of the platform, the recruits folded their hands and bowed their heads. Recruit Sing was distantly aware of what the chaplain was saying. Recruit Sing stared at the eagle, globe, and anchor in her hand. It was a simple diecast, flat black metal pin. It was all Recruit Sing could do to keep from tearing up. She had made it. She had joined an organization that was larger than herself and had proven herself worthy of acceptance into that organization. Private Cassandra Sing, USMC studied every curve and cut of her new emblem.

The recruits around her muttered, "Amen."

Private Sing looked up at the platform.

The senior drill instructor shouted, "Marines, you are out of uniform! Affix your eagle, globe, and anchor on your eight-point cover."

The group's energy returned in waves. Reserved excitement spread amongst the new Marines as they put their pins on their hats. They shared quiet smiles, muted laughs, and mutual congratulations. Private Sing wasn't as tired as she had been. The other new Marines showed more sparkle as well. Private Sing didn't notice the sand in her hair as she placed her newly adorned cover back on her head. She tilted the cover forward just a little more because she stood just a little taller. She shared smiles and nods with her new comrades-in-arms. She was a fully trained, fully certified, but as yet, an untested Marine.

"Gear up," the senior drill instructor shouted. "Battalion, atten...tion!"

Private Sing balanced her weapon in the crook of her hip as she hoisted her field pack onto her shoulders. The chafes on her shoulders weren't as bad as they had been. They were insignificant, really. They would heal. She closed the chest clasp and didn't feel the tender skin on her ribs.

When the Marines were all at attention, the senior drill instructor ordered, "All right, Marines, you have completed the Crucible. We're going to re-enter the main base. Are you going to drag in like a bunch of whipped raw recruits or are we going to make an entrance like the Marine Corps' newest Marines? Do I hear an 'Oorah'?"

"Oorah!"

"Port... arms! Left... face!"

Private Sing's rifle seemed to weigh nothing. When she turned to the left, the pain in her calves wasn't worth mentioning. Her thighs were strong and steady again.

"Forward... march!"

Her stress and fatigue of the last three days drained out of her body and onto the road. All the minor annoyances that she felt before were gone. She ignored the protests of her right knee. The strain was minor. At that moment, Private Sing felt as though she could have turned around and performed the Crucible a second time if the drill instructors so ordered.

"Double time... march!" the senior drill instructor ordered.

Cassie intoned, *Right step, left step, run.*

The air around Private Sing was no longer humid and heavy. Her running created a breeze on her face. The morning air was cool and tasted sweet. Private Sing was still hungry, but she would survive. As the two companies turned onto the road, Private Sing knew what lay ahead of them the rest of the afternoon. They would clean and check their weapons at the armory for the last time. They would drop their gear at the barracks and go to the mess hall to partake in the Warrior's Dinner.

The Warrior's Dinner was how the Marine Corps acknowledged the completion of the Crucible. At the dinner, the new Marines could take as long as they wanted to eat their meal. The mess hall staff prepared every food in their inventory for the event. The Marines could eat as much as they wanted, which could be a lot after two days in the Crucible, and eat anything they wanted, including all the forbidden foods like ice cream and carbonated drinks. They could even talk during the festivities and be boisterous. Private Sing could almost taste the strawberry ice cream.

The first few recruits of Alpha Company emerged from the last copse of trees and onto the Paris Island main base. The new company of Marines made its grand entrance after the Crucible.

The senior drill instructor called the running cadence that would alert the entire base that new Marines were returning to base. When Private Sing emerged from the tree line, she saw the faces of recruits turned toward them. She called cadence even louder. She looked to her far right and saw the gas chamber. She watched a small group of male recruits walk in a tight circle with their arms stretched out to their sides and their heads bowed. The cool air tasted sweeter.

*****

Cassie lay back on her pillow. She moved her arm to a more comfortable position. She had been quiet for some time and didn't know what to say.

Uncle Brian broke the silence. "Believe it or not, that good cry was the best thing that you could do for yourself. If it happens again, let it rip. If you want to talk, you can always call me." He smiled.

Cassie had to admit that she felt as if the burden of stress was gone. A nurse followed by a phlebotomist walked into the room and broke the moment.

"Excuse us, Mr. Sing, but I have some nursing to attend to and Tim needs to draw some blood. Can I ask you to step outside for a moment?" She looked past Brian and smiled radiantly.

"Sure. I'll be outside."

Before Brian could slide off the edge of the bed, Cassie spoke up. "Uncle Brian, do you mind if we call it a night. I'm tired. We can talk more tomorrow."

"Of course. I'll come by in the morning."

Brian smiled at the nurse and asked, "What time will you be receiving guests in the morning?"

The nurse switched to tour-guide mode and answered, "Well, we have twenty-four-hour visitation, except when we're working, but breakfast is from seven to nine. You could join her for breakfast."

Brian looked to Cassie for her preference.

"Breakfast would be great. See you in the morning, Uncle Brian.

When they were alone, the technician drew the evening's samples, and the nurse took Cassie's vitals. When they finished, the nurse handed Cassie a small paper cup with an assortment of pills in it.

As the nurse poured some water into Cassie's cup, Cassie asked, "What are all these?"

The nurse looked at Cassie as though there was a conspiracy surrounding the pills and said, "Those are doctor's orders. One's an antibiotic. One's a blood thinner. There is an anti-nausea agent, an anti-inflammatory, and a pill for the pain. What is your pain level, one to ten?"

"My pain is pretty low. Would I be breaking the rules if I passed on the pain pill and the sleeping pill? I don't like the loss of control that I get when I take most pain medications."

The nurse produced a second paper cup and put the pain and sleeping pills in it. "I'll keep it at the nurse's station. If you change your mind later, buzz me."

Cassie took her remaining pills. The nurse turned the lights down and left. Cassie turned over, away from her wounds, and tried to get comfortable. She was facing the door to her room, but a privacy curtain blocked the top half of the open door. Light from the hallway showed under the curtain. She listened to the sounds of the nurses coming and going from the various rooms and to the chatter at the nurses' station. The trickle of sound was relaxing, like the sound of waves on a beach or rain on a tin roof. Cassie looked at the digital clock--8:29 p.m. Cassie took a deep breath, closed her eyes, let her breath out slowly, and slept.

She didn't register that it had been twenty-four hours almost to the minute since she had seen the lights come on at the Fort Sill north gate.

Chapter Thirty-Three

Cassie woke up at 11:00. She was restless, uncomfortable, and still had a dull headache. She fluffed her pillows, tugged at her blankets, turned on her side, and huffed and puffed. After ten minutes of this, Cassie resigned herself to the fact that she wasn't going to get back to sleep until she got up, walked the halls, and worked out some of the kinks. She pushed the button to call the duty nurse who arrived in seconds.

"Yes? How are you doing? Is it time for that pain pill or sleep aid?"

"No, thanks; I'll pass. I do have a bit of a headache, though. I'd like to walk around the hallway loop to burn off some energy, though. Would that be all right?"

As Cassie talked, she sat up and slung her legs over the side of the bed. The maneuver wasn't easy with one arm. The wound in her side had some pain, but not as much as Cassie expected.

The nurse lowered the bed's side rail and answered, "Sure. The more you can be up and around the better. Do you want to visit the ladies' room first?"

"I don't think so." Cassie made a motion to stand up. Her legs went rubbery, and she started to sink. She sat back again and said, "I'm a little wobbly. Maybe I'd better take the walker."

Cassie walked past a couple of other patient rooms before she said, "This feels better. I was going stir crazy being confined to that bed. I know it's the middle of the night, but when we get back, can I sit up in the chair for a while?"

"Sure! That'd be good for you."

Cassie's left wrist trembled. Her first thought was that the tremor was from the strain of walking. She looked at the far end of the hallway where it turned to the other side of the ward. If she made it that far, she'd cross to the other side of the ward and come back on the other side. She thought of her walks as laps around the track. She wanted out of the hospital, so the more active she was, the better.

The nurse said something, but Cassie couldn't understand her. Her words were all jumbled. The end of the hallway receded as if someone had spun the zoom knob on a camera. Pain exploded in the back of her skull. It felt as if someone hit her with a hot baseball bat. Nausea overwhelmed her. She wanted to throw up but couldn't. She couldn't speak. She couldn't even turn her head. She felt herself sinking to the floor. The last sensation she had was that of arms encircling her body.

She heard the nurse yell, "I need a gurney here!"

*****

"Cassie! Cassie!"

Someone out in the fog was calling her name. She thought that she answered, "What?" aloud, but she couldn't be sure.

The insistent voice came again, "Cassie, open your eyes."

She thought, *Okay.*

Opening her eyes was easier. She opened her eyes as little as she could and let the bright lights in. She winced.

The voice said, "Can we turn the lights down? Hey, Short Stuff, welcome back."

She turned her head toward the voice. She knew who it was. Only her Uncle Brian was brave enough to call her Short Stuff. Her head felt bruised, not painful but like the bruise that comes after the pain. She focused on the face.

"Uncle Brian."

"How are you feeling? You gave us quite a scare last night."

"I feel like a can of mashed …" She didn't finish because she remembered that her mother didn't like her using the colorful 'mashed assholes' phrase. She reworded her answer, "I've felt better. What happened?"

A nurse on one side placed a blood pressure cuff on her wrist and started it. A nurse on the other leaned in and flashed a light in her eyes one at a time.

Brian took a step back as the nurses worked. "It seems as if the bump on your head did a bit more damage than the doctors had initially diagnosed. You had a small brain bleed, but the doctors took care of it. You're out of the woods. The surgeon should be here in a minute. I'll let him explain it to you. You just rest right now."

One of the nurses placed two of her fingers across the palm of Cassie's hand, "Squeeze my fingers. Other side. Good. You look great. Any nausea?"

Cassie was sipping ice water twenty minutes later when the doctor walked in.

"Good morning, Corporal Sing. My name is Colonel Oro. I performed your surgery last night. How are you feeling? You look like you're recovering nicely, good color, vitals are good. Follow my pen without moving your head. Good. Any nausea?"

"When I woke up, but I'm better now. I'm hungry."

Dr. Oro put down the chart he was reading. "Well, we'll just have to do something about that." He turned to one of the nurses and ordered, "Clear liquids. If she keeps them down, she will go to a bland diet. I'll reevaluate this evening."

Cassie waited until the doctor finished talking and then asked, "What happened?"

"At some point in your ordeal a couple of nights ago, you got a good bump on the back of your head. It didn't cause us any concerns. At the time, nothing showed up on the X-Rays. It turns out that you had a small bleed between the layers of tissue that surrounds your brain. The bleed itself was minor. However, as the pocket of blood grew, it pressed on the tissues around the brain and, ultimately, on the brain itself. It was so small and slow growing that it took twenty-four hours to manifest itself. Even last night, the hematoma was hard to find on an x-ray. We drilled a small hole in the back of your head and relieved the pressure. Your vitals returned to normal almost instantly. As near as we can tell, the bleeding has stopped. In case you were wondering, it was a tiny hole and only took one stitch.

"You were lucky. You were walking next to the best nurse in the hospital. Her quick, accurate diagnosis and call to me kept the trauma minor. She saved you a lot of potential problems."

As the doctor spoke, a nurse stepped up to stand next to the doctor. Cassie recognized her from the night before. Cassie smiled and mouthed, "Thanks!"

The doctor continued, "We're going to keep you here a couple of extra days for observation. Judging by how well you're doing this morning, it may be a complete waste of time, but I want to be extra cautious and make sure that you're out of the woods." He placed a hand on Cassie's forearm and smiled his most reassuring smile. "I'll come by to check on you this evening. You just keep doing what you're doing. You're recovering nicely. This whole ordeal is nearly over."

The doctor left the room.

Brian watched the doctor leave the room before he said, "Well, it looks like you might be here for a couple of days." He reached for Cassie's laptop and cell phone. He opened the computer and said, "You have ninety-one emails and a week's worth of Facebook. Where do you want to start?"

As Brian read the first email aloud, a member of the food services staff walked in with a food tray. There were several assorted juices, a large cup of chicken bouillon, a large cup of beef bouillon, and an empty cup for mixing.

Chapter Thirty-Four

Two weeks after Cassie's discharge, Duane Connors stood on the front porch of Happy's Quick-Mart and Bait Shop just outside of Medicine Park. Duane suggested the bait shop as a good meeting place when Cassie had called a few nights ago.

Cassie had finished her Nuclear Weapons Firefighting rotation at Fort Sill and would be processing out and leaving Oklahoma in a couple of days. If Duane and Cassie were going to have a beer and regale his friends with tales of their car wreck (the DHS cover story) in the Oklahoma outback, it would have to be today.

Duane scanned the cars as they pulled into the parking lot, looking for any young woman that looked like a Marine. He had only seen Cassie once, on a back road in the deserted hills of Oklahoma at midnight. They had talked on the phone a few times and had exchanged emails, but he wasn't sure that he'd be able to pick her out of a crowd.

Duane was checking his watch for the twentieth time when a blood red and Navy blue (once a Marine, always a Marine) Kawasaki Super Sport motorcycle rumbled into the parking lot. Duane checked the bike out first and then noticed the impossibly small female rider. When she took off her helmet, he saw the tight, regulation Marine Corps hair bun.

This must be Cassie. This can't be Cassie. OMG, that tiny thing is a Lance Corporal firefighter in the Marines?

This girl couldn't be over five-foot-five and was powerful like a dancer. She moved like a cat. She maneuvered the motorcycle around as though it was no heavier than an acoustic guitar.

Duane thought *she belongs at a debutante's ball, not in combat boots. She's a fox.*

Where was the drill sergeant who accosted him on a back road a couple of weeks ago? Where was the military demeanor and commanding presence that had forced his compliance for their mission?

Cassie's smile melted him. All he could do was smile back.

"Hi, Duane, it's nice to see you again," she said. "Things sure look different in the daylight, don't they?"

"Hi, Cassie. They sure do. Welcome to Happy's."

Cassie knew that there would be a small crowd of Duane's friends inside waiting for Cassie. She wanted to take a minute and visit with Duane alone. She also wanted to remind him of some of the classified subjects that he couldn't bring up.

"Can we sit a minute before we go in?"

"Sure," Duane gestured to a pair of rustic, tree-limb chairs set out for the tourists. "What's up?"

"Before we go in, I just wanted to take a minute and see how you're doing. Everything going okay?" she asked with a touch of "close friend" in her voice. They had been through an ordeal together. She felt a bond with Duane that only people who have experienced such an ordeal could understand.

"Sure," Duane answered." As I said before, the Army kept me around for the better part of the next day. But they treated me well. There are a couple of things that happened since we last talked."

Cassie raised her brows in interest.

"I received a small federal reward for assisting in the identification and capture of a terrorist cell. I now have a new phone with a new battery and a car charger. I also have a working rifle in my truck if you ever need to borrow it."

Cassie smiled.

"Also, I got a call from the Army recruiter in Lawton asking me to come in and talk to him if I'm still interested in enlisting. I have an appointment on Monday. He said that I still had to complete my GED, but for me not to worry about my lack of college credits. It seems that a personal letter of recommendation from a Major General Omar Marks, Fourth Army Command carries a lot of weight."

"Nice," Cassie said and then waited for Duane to go on.

"I'd like to be a rescue helicopter pilot."

"Oorah," Cassie added in a quiet but complimentary voice, and she stuck out her fist for a bump.

"How about you, have you found out where you're going next?"

"Actually, yes I have, and it's not classified. My next assignment is the Base Fire Brigade at the Marine Corps Air Station in Kunioko, Japan. From there, the Marines will send me on a temporary duty status to the next rotation of Marine Corps EMS training. Command also offered me a slot at the next class at Officers Candidate School, but I'm more of an in-the-field, action, adrenaline junkie. I'm going to go for the Marine Corps EMT training."

"Oorah," Duane said, parroting Cassie's earlier compliment.

"Oorah."

After a short, awkward pause, Cassie asked, "So, what's a lady got to do to get a cold Blue Moon around here?"

Duane recovered his composure. He still couldn't believe that this woman was in the Marines.

"Come on inside," Duane smiled his best James Dean smile and opened the swinging door for Cassie.

As Duane entered the main part of the store ahead of Cassie, he shouted toward the back, "Max, everybody, this is the soldier that I told you about."

Cassie smiled her most gregarious smile as she walked to the back of the store and waited for Max to appear.

Lance Corporal Cassandra Sing, USMC corrected Duane's faux pas.

"Marine. I'm a Marine."

Epilogue

The day after Cassie met with Duane, the local Lawton, Oklahoma newspaper, The Constitution, ran a one-inch single column article on page six, below the fold:

The U.S. Army released information about the explosion that some residents of rural Oklahoma saw two weeks ago. An Army truck carrying propane tanks for an Army field kitchen caught fire and exploded on a highway, fifty-five miles northwest of Fort Sill. The Army credits the driver's quick action in driving the truck off the main highway with minimizing the damage caused by the explosion. The blast destroyed the truck. The Army reports that no military personnel were hurt in the incident.

Jeff Bailey

I hope you enjoyed my story. We authors, live by online reviews. I would very much appreciate if you would take some time and post a review on a couple of the more influential sites:

Amazon.com

GoodReads.com

BarnesAndNoble.com

If you are unfamiliar with the process for posting reviews, email me:

jeff.bailey4007@gmail.com

I will talk you through it. I always enjoy hearing from a fan.

Also, if you decide not to keep this book in your personal library, please, don't discard it. Pass it on to someone else that might enjoy the read. Thanks for your time.

--Jeff

__The Chilcoat Project__

Chapter One

The Marie Curie National Laboratory outside Seattle, Washington occupied a dispersed footprint in the beautiful, tranquil, pine forest overlooking the Puget Sound. To fit into the wooded setting without disturbing any of the trees, the MCN (everyone called the Madam Curie National Laboratory the MCN) occupied thirty-four random buildings bound together into a 'research campus.' The campus looked more like a scattering of unrelated electronics businesses than one of the nation's premier laser and nuclear research facilities. The surrounding residents were unaware how much DOD (Department of Defense) and DARPA (Defense Advanced Research Program Administration) research the MCN conducted in these inconspicuous campus buildings.

There didn't seem to be any security surrounding the campus. There was no perimeter fence and no hundred yards of flat, rocky, vegetation-free, no-man's-land surrounding the fence. In fact, any local resident could park in any of the Campus parking lots, use the outdoor picnic areas (which they do), or walk up to the outside doors of any of the lab buildings without being challenged.

The campus did have the latest generation key card electronic building security. Every outside door of every MCN building was also equipped with a hi-res surveillance camera. A duty security officer at the main security center could monitor the foot traffic in the immediate area around every outside door of any building in the MCN complex. A huge web of area security cameras, in little black domes, high up on buildings, and on the tops of parking lot light poles supplemented the door security camera. In addition, several pairs of lab security personnel patrolled the campus grounds, 24/7. Of course, roving patrols are only effective when they happen to be in the right place at the right time. Camera surveillance is no more effective than the people monitoring the system feeds. Recorded images only provide incriminating information if a live person reviews the images.

The Spectroscopy Laser Lab, SLL, was a sprawling one-story building on the northern outskirts of the campus. The SLL was a world-war-two era building and looked its age. The ground level of the SLL was all office space, but lab scientists conducted a wide array of classified research in the two basement levels. The research conducted in the SLL involved lasers and how lasers interacted with the molecules of selected materials: mostly nuclear materials. The U.S. military, DARPA, and the DHS selected the materials for the research. It was rumored (even inside the lab, it was rumored) that much of the work on the Star Wars Satellite Defense System was developed in the SLL's labs. Most of the senior MCN staff who work at the SLL also knew that the Laser Weapons System (LaWS) was developed in the basements of the SLL. The LaWS weapon is the latest and most effective ship-mounted laser defense system deployed by the US Navy.

Outdoor camera security for the SLL was excellent. Cameras mounted on the roof gave overlapping fields of vision that covered the roof and the outer grounds. Parking lot cameras covered the outsides of the building, the bulk of the parking lots and the other cameras. Smaller cameras mounted on the extreme corners of the building gave a close-up view of the grounds close to the buildings. Dedicated camera surveillance covered the back door and the loading bay of the SLL. The parking lot had no less than six cameras focused on it at all times. However, one small corner of the parking lot didn't receive as much coverage as it should have. Only one panning camera scanned the three or four parking slots closest to the building by the loading bay. In addition, this panning camera could scan the back half of these parking places at the extreme limit of the panning cycle. Part of the building's structure blocked the total view. Even then, the panning camera focused on these parking places for a mere three seconds out of every thirty. Then, the panning camera panned away to the rest of the parking lot. Even the loading dock cameras were around the corner from these parking places. Beyond the unmonitored parking places was a small, secondary driveway opened into the residential housing area behind the SLL. This driveway was unmonitored.

At 5:50 a.m. on a Friday morning in May, an unmarked, unremarkable white service van drove out of the residential area behind the SLL and turned into the small service driveway. In an easy, unhurried way, the driver parked in the end parking place closest to the loading bay. The driver got into the back where he had an unobstructed view of the parking lot through the tinted windows.

The passenger got out of the van and dropped a bundle of twenty-dollar bills held together by a paper clip on the ground next to the van's sliding door. Then, he stepped around to the front of the van to wait. There was no noticeable traffic in this area of the SLL's parking lot. It was Friday and half of the lab personnel were on their alternating Friday off. It was also before 6:00 a.m., and few of the staff, engineers, or scientist started work that early.

At 6:00 a.m. sharp, senior scientist Moses Chilcoat drove into the SLL parking lot in his rundown little twenty-year-old BMW. It had rained the night before, and the air smelled crisp, clean, and refreshing, with a slight aftertaste of wet garden. Moses' always arrived at work by 6:00 a.m. and always parked in the last parking place by the loading dock. His office was the first office off the hallway just inside the loading bay. Across from his office, a keycard protected stairwell led to the labs on the first basement level. Moses's lab was adjacent to that stairwell on the first basement level, beneath his office. Everything was close, convenient. It sure beat the long walk from the building's main entrance.

Moses could slide his ID card thru the magnetic card scanner and press his thumb on the fingerprint reader to open the personnel door beside the main loading dock roll-up door. On occasion, a voice from the little black dome asked Moses to face the camera for a visual identification. It still beat the long walk from the front door.

Even though it wasn't quite daylight, Moses could see the problem ahead of him. Someone had parked a white van in his parking place. Moses looked at the white van in amazement. Most people don't park that far from the front entrance. What, once or twice a year, someone was parked in his *private* parking place. Moses decided that the three extra steps wouldn't hurt him, so he parked next to the van. He stepped out of his car and took a deep breath. He loved the cool, musty forest air in the morning. As he closed his car door, a man stepped from in front of the van, smiled, and whispered, "Excuse me, Sir, you dropped something." He gestured to the ground at Moses' feet. A small bundle of twenty-dollar bills lay on the wet asphalt at his feet.

As Moses started to bend down to retrieve his good fortune, the man stepped in closer and grabbed Moses' forearm in a steel grip. Moses's first thought was that the man was trying to punch him in the gut and Moses grunted a little as he tried to turn away. Behind Moses, the vans side door slid open, and the second man pulled a mesh-cloth hood over Moses's head and cinched it tight around his neck. Moses lurched back against his assailant. It wasn't a defensive move, as much as Moses simply slipped on the wet pavement. Moses started to bring his free arm up in front of him to try to keep from falling.

The assailant in front of Moses held a stun gun in his right hand. He had been trying to stun Moses, not punch him and had not been as successful as he had wanted. Moses had been stunned enough to make him uncoordinated but not enough to incapacitate him. When Moses raised his arm, the assailant thought that Moses was fighting back, and this perceived resistance angered the man. As many of his associates had learned the painful way, the man had a quick and violent temper. His superiors had admonished him on many occasions for releasing it. Even the members of his cell were cautious not to trigger his outbursts.

Today, he decided not to comply. He kneed Moses in the groin with as much viciousness and power as he could muster. The force almost lifted Moses off the ground, and the pain erased all remaining thoughts of resistance from Moses's mind. When Moses came down, he crumpled to the ground like a limp, wet newspaper and felt the puddled rainwater from the parking lot seep through the side of his hood and onto his face.

Two pairs of hands snatched Moses from the ground and tossed him into the cargo area of the van. One of his assailants followed him in while the other closed the sliding door, picked up the money, and returned to the driver's door. Moses landed on the van's bare metal cargo floor, face down, hard. The assailant pressed an elbow across his neck and in a voice that was no more than a whisper, said, 'Make a sound, and I'll kill you.' The assailant's choice of words encouraged the clueless Moses because it implied that if Moses cooperated, he might live. The assailant sucker punched Moses in the kidneys, for emphasis.

Whether from exhaustion (great physical prowess was not one of Moses' personal traits), abject fear, or debilitating pain, Moses couldn't make enough sound to answer the threat. Moses assumed that these men were professionals. He remembered from MCN security-training videos on executive abduction that whispered voices were impossible to identify. Whispered voices are anonymous. Moses stayed quiet and didn't try to move. If these men were whispering, he reassured himself that they must plan to let him go after they got what they wanted. They didn't want Moses to be able to identify them. Moses registered a slight pinch as his assailant injected him in the butt cheek with a sedative.

As Moses lost consciousness, the driver started the van and backed out of the parking place with careful deliberation. He drove out of the parking lot at no more than twenty-five miles per hour and turned to the right into the residential neighborhood behind the SLL. A block away, the driver parked and put two magnetic signs advertising a carpet cleaning service on the sides of the van. Peace and quiet had returned to the SLL parking lot. After fifty-four seconds of frantic violence against Moses, everything was calm again. Forest tranquility had returned. No one in the building had seen anything. There was no one else in the parking lot. No camera had recorded the assault. Even the ever-present raucous birds in the canopy of trees hadn't been disturbed. Fifty-four seconds had passed since Moses had closed his car door. Moses Chilcoat, the super-educated fair-haired scientific prodigy of the MCN, was gone.

Made in the USA
Middletown, DE
15 August 2024